I0573781

Colleen's Choice

Emerald Springs Legacy Book Two

HOLLEY TRENT
author of *A Demon in Waiting*

CRIMSON
ROMANCE

F+W Media, Inc.

Copyright © 2014 by Holley Trent.
All rights reserved.
This book, or parts thereof, may not be reproduced in any form without permission
from the publisher; exceptions are made for brief excerpts used in published reviews.

Published by
Crimson Romance
an imprint of F+W Media, Inc.
10151 Carver Road, Suite 200
Blue Ash, OH 45242. U.S.A.
www.crimsonromance.com

ISBN 10: 1-4405-7099-X
ISBN 13: 978-1-4405-7099-5
eISBN 10: 1-4405-7100-7
eISBN 13: 978-1-4405-7100-8

This is a work of fiction. Names, characters, corporations, institutions, organizations,
events, or locales in this novel are either the product of the author's imagination or, if
real, used fictitiously. The resemblance of any character to actual persons (living or dead)
is entirely coincidental.

Cover art © designpics/123RF; iStockphoto.com/M_a_y_a:

CHAPTER ONE

Colleen Sanders took a bracing breath before mashing the last few digits of the number she never expected to dial again. Slinking off her seat edge, she took sanctuary beneath her abused cherry desk, gripping the edge of her phone base as she went.

Her father had stripped the carpet from the big office two years past and had never gotten around to replacing it. The staff lingering in the hall could probably hear every blink—every whisper—even through her closed door.

She curled into the corner, drawing her knees up to her chin as her target picked up his extension.

"Greg Quinton."

"Greg. Hi." She swallowed the lump in her throat and lowered her voice to a whisper. "How are you?"

"Great. That you, Colleen? Sounds like your rasp."

"Yeah, it's me."

"Was just thinking about you—talking about you, actually—at the retreat last week. Miss you around here."

She pinched the bridge of her nose between her thumb and forefinger, and mentally berated herself for her lachrymose tendencies as of late. Ball-busting Colleen had never been a crier. She hadn't even cried during that one lacrosse match freshman year when a freak collision resulted in her dislocated shoulder and broken nose, although she had introduced the Emerald Springs residents in attendance to the less refined components of her vocabulary. The official had tossed her a yellow card for that outburst. She'd framed it.

"Miss all of you, too," she confessed.

"Hey, can you speak up? I can hardly hear you."

"No. Listen, do you … " She closed her eyes and willed her churning gut to calm. This was just *Greg*. Out of all the calls she'd had to make in recent weeks, this should have been an easy one. Another deep breath. "Listen, do you have any work for me?"

"Work?"

There was surprise in Greg's voice, and Colleen couldn't tell if it was pleasant or otherwise.

"Yes. Got any design work for me?"

A pause. Greg rustled some papers on his end of the call in Seattle, and there was a thump, followed by a loud, squealing whine.

Colleen yanked the phone back from her ear and held it away until the infernal racket ceased.

Greg came back on the line. "Sorry! Sorry."

Colleen put the phone back against her ear and whispered, "What happened?"

"Got so excited I dropped the phone. We're short some boot designs and have been in a frenzy trying to develop new motifs. I'm pretty sure the timing of your phone call is in direct response to the bargains I made with at least three pagan gods last night."

Her shoulders fell with her relief, and she blew out a breath. "Can you pay me up-front?"

Another pause. "How are things at the farm? Any better?"

"No." Why bother explaining? Greg already knew the dirt.

"Damn. Hey, I'll walk the invoice up to accounting right now. We'll try to get the check cut before FedEx gets here. I'll send you specs as soon as I'm back at my desk."

"Greg, thank you. Really. Thank you. You're getting me out of some serious hot water."

He laughed, and Colleen heard the sound of his heels clacking against the concrete floors at the Markson Outfitters corporate headquarters. Already on the move, Greg was. Colleen had learned a lot about efficiency working under that guy for all those years.

"Pays to have friends in high places, huh?" he asked. "Don't worry about it. You're doing me a massive favor. When you see the deadline, you'll understand."

Colleen laughed, too, and couldn't remember the last time she'd heard that sound coming out of her mouth. Things in her life hadn't been conducive to laughter in the past few months. "Thanks for the warning. I'll look for your email."

"Bye, love."

She put the phone in its base and crawled out from her hidey-hole. No sooner had she'd pulled up to her feet than the phone rang again, the display flashing an interoffice extension. She sighed and set the phone on the desktop before stabbing the speaker button. "Yes, Kate?"

"Colleen, you have some visitors here to see you," her secretary said.

Damn it. Kate had her on speakerphone on her end, too. That meant her dependable assistant had probably already told whoever it was that Colleen was unavailable, but they had insisted on having an audience. She couldn't bluff her way out of this visit as easily as she had with Sam Whitman earlier in the morning. Sam—marketing director at the neighboring Emerald Tea Farm—wasn't there to pay her any money, and she sure as shit didn't owe them any, so in her book, a meeting was unnecessary. Mercenary, true, but she couldn't turn Split Acres Farm around if she was on her ass engaging in idle chitchat all day. As it was, she was already digging the farm out of a grave that was filling in faster than she could shovel clear.

"And who are the visitors?" she asked, rubbing the bridge of her nose again.

"The septic tank contractor has finished his work and wants to talk to you … and Alan's here."

"Who's Alan?"

Kate had said "Alan" in manner indicating Colleen should already know that. She didn't.

"I ... think you should talk to him."

That didn't sound good. Did she owe someone a paycheck and had forgotten?

No, that couldn't be it. She'd been staring over the foreman's shoulder for four weeks, approving every timecard to make sure he didn't let any overtime slip in. She'd issued pay for every single one of those hours.

"Fine. Let me just ... " she opened and shut her desk drawer twice. " ... finish up the filing I'm doing, and I'll be right out."

"Yes, ma'am." Kate clicked off.

"Damn it." The matronly assistant never called Colleen "ma'am" unless the situation required a certain performance. It was their unofficial code word.

Colleen shoved her socked feet into the powder blue floral-print rain boots awaiting her near the door and used the small mirror hung over the file cabinets to smooth the lumps from her hair. If someone suggested she had dressed in the dark that morning, the statement wouldn't have been so far from the truth. Being in a perpetual state of exhaustion, she rarely had her eyes open before arriving at Split Acres Farm's operations office, and Kate had poured that first pot of coffee down her gullet. Further, her lights were on the fritz at the old house. Sometimes they worked, sometimes they didn't, and sometimes she got a shock. Literally.

She looked haggard in that reflection. Until recently, she'd looked her age, maybe a little under it. She got good genes from her mother's side, but from her father's side, she got a major headache in the form of four hundred acres of unprofitable farmland. She was thirty-two but feeling pretty damn close to retirement age. No wonder her mother had always been so tired when Colleen and her brother, Jacob, were growing up. There was just so much to do, and she was doing it with far less staff than her parents ever had.

Oh well. She wasn't trying to win a sash and tiara. She just needed to deal with two visitors as efficiently and painlessly as possible.

She straightened her spine, smoothed her expression into the unreadable blank she always met the public with, and pulled open the door.

Showtime.

She was already talking before she'd cleared the end of the long corridor of mostly empty offices, and had her hand extended for the contractor to shake. "Thanks for coming out so fast, Bart." She caught a glimpse of a tall, dark-haired man lingering near the entryway, but she let him remain in her periphery for the time being. One thing at a time.

Bart switched his clipboard to his left hand and wrapped his big, rough, right hand around hers. "You should have called weeks ago when the plumbing started backing up. Would have been less of a problem."

She was perfectly aware of that. Less of a problem, but no less expensive to fix.

"Everything is in working order, then? Tanks are empty?"

He nodded and handed the clipboard over to her. He crooked his thumb toward the door. "Your custodian here looked it over and said it was fine. Signed off on the work. I just need a check."

All the words made sense. They were English, after all, but they didn't seem to apply to her particular situation. She squared her shoulders and cocked up her favored eyebrow. "I'm sorry?"

Bart took the clipboard back and pointed to something printed in the terms. "Payable upon completion. I guess you don't have a line of credit?"

Her teeth clenched, and she sucked a sobering breath through her nose. *Damn you, Daddy.* She'd waited as long as she did to call them in the first place because she expected to have money to pay the bill in the thirty days it took it to come due. Now she'd have to go rob Peter to pay Paul again.

She took the clipboard back and raised her chin, hoping to garner some sense of authority in the situation, but on the inside she was crumbling. Mess after mess, it never let up. How much more could she take?

"And my *custodian* signed off on it, you said?" She brought the paper up to her eyes and squinted at the scrawled signature. Alan … something-or-other.

Finally, she gave the man more than just her peripheral vision. She stared at him dead-on, expecting him to flinch and blanch like all the others did, but he lifted a hand in greeting and grinned.

Her jaw fell open, and she was stunned momentarily by the blue of his eyes, his chiseled jaw, his dark hair—deliciously unkempt and tickling the top of his collar—and the strong forearms her eyes skimmed down to as he twirled a ratchet wrench between long, tanned fingers.

A stranger, and if she had to guess, her father was to blame for him being there. Why did he agree to let her come home and do the job if he wasn't going to get out of the way to let her do it?

She closed her mouth and swallowed, turning her attention back to Bart. "Have a seat. I'll go cut you a check."

Bart shrugged, shuffled across the worn carpet, and plopped into one of the vinyl chairs near the door.

"Alan," she said, spinning on her boot heel and striding toward the hall. "Why don't you join me in my office and tell me about the work while I run this check through QuickBooks?"

"Yes, certainly, Colleen."

She stumbled a bit over her own feet, glad that no one, beyond the corporate sheltie lounging brazenly in the middle of the hall, could see it. She stepped over the dog and concentrated on her breathing as she approached her office.

Dear lord, he had an accent.

Get a grip, woman.

By the time she plopped her butt in her desk chair and punched her computer monitor button, her supposed custodian joined her in the office, and the blush inching up her neck had receded.

"Close the door, please."

He gave her a speculative look but put his hand on the doorknob and pushed.

She ducked her head behind her computer monitor, clicking her mouse blindly at nothing in particular. She couldn't see straight for some reason, and she didn't think it was low blood sugar.

Gorgeous man. Too bad she'd have to fire him.

CHAPTER TWO

So, this was the woman who had the Split Acres staff mentioning her only in hushed tones as if she were omnipresent? The one her own father had warned him would probably have him off the job before he'd even gotten started? The one Adam Whitman had suggested he query for employment, but who'd also cringed as the name passed his lips?

Cold Colleen, they'd called her.

Ha.

Her fingers, draped over her computer mouse, quavered with each click—each swipe across the pad. Her pink lips, pressed into a tight line, occasionally twitched at the corners. Her eyes—a deep, dark brown that reminded him of fecund soil and roasted coffee beans—were a bit too round for a woman who was all business and no heart. Maybe no one else could see it because they weren't looking. They saw Colleen as a woman in authority; a woman from whom they needed things. A woman who could say no, and with that tiny little word, devastate their plans. Of course they'd see her as some kind of statue.

The Colleen he saw—this tired slip of a woman—may have been in control, but she was definitely losing herself to it. He saw it because he didn't need anything from her, not really.

She didn't scare him one whit.

She cleared her throat and the laser printer at the far corner whined to life, warming up as she rolled across the room and pulled out the paper tray. She slipped a blank check into the feeder and closed the flap before turning her attention to him.

"You've taken me a bit by surprise," she said, staring across the desk at him beneath heavy eyelids. "Last I knew, we didn't have a custodian."

"Your father hired me."

She performed a slow nod—a nod that was easy enough to translate into the implied *duh* she was likely thinking.

The check whirred through the machine and Colleen wheeled her rolling chair back to the printer to fetch it. "I'm going to be candid so you understand I'm just not a woman on a power trip."

"Please do." He liked a woman to shoot straight from the hip. Saved time that way.

"I imagine you were hired around Monday of last week?"

"Yes."

"Figures. The one day I actually decided to be sick in my own bed instead of sick at work, Daddy makes a hire behind my back." She clucked her tongue, shook her head, and uncapped a black pen on her desk. With a flourish, she signed the check and stood. "Be right back. Gotta pay a guy."

"Yes, of course." Alan moved sideways out of the path of the door after pulling it open for his agitated employer.

She stomped past him, check in hand, leaving the smell of coffee and gardenias in her wake.

He grinned. Coffee. In the short time he'd been in the area, he'd found the residents had a distinct preference for tea, given one of the largest organic growers in the country was situated in their community. He'd come to Emerald Springs hoping to find a job at the tea farm, but they were fully staffed in any of the positions he would take. He was a bit overqualified to be a picker. He figured he'd bide his time at the neighboring Split Acres until he could transition, but the longer he stayed, the more he wondered if perhaps there was something about this rundown operation its spit-shined competitor didn't have. From great tragedy comes great triumph, the saying went, and this place definitely fit the loose definition of tragic. He'd seen prisons with more verve.

He rubbed his hand over his day's growth of stubble and pondered it. Yeah. Maybe he needed to think bigger.

Colleen returned nearly as quickly as she'd left and shut the door without regarding him. She sank into her chair and waved him forward.

He pulled back one of the metal folding chairs in front of her desk and eyed it.

"They're sound, I promise," she said with a sigh.

He sat but didn't exhale until he was certain his ass wouldn't meet the floor.

"Daddy had started redecorating in here a couple of years ago. Sold everything but this desk, and then changed his mind because he got busy."

"Busy is usually a good thing."

She blew air though her flattened lips, sputtering them like a motorboat engine. "Yes, usually, but in this case he got busy with other interests. Ran for a seat in the state legislature and won it. He and Mom live in Olympia when the Senate is in session. Comes home about once a week to raise hell and throw monkey wrenches into my operation, as you can see."

Ouch. "Your operation?"

She narrowed her eyes and huffed. "Oh yeah. Little-known secret. I own about forty percent of this Eden. That's part of the reason why I'm here and not in Seattle where I had a life and friends other than the ones who live in the Internet."

So, the ballsy boss actually had some power? Interesting. He shifted the wrench he'd been toying with to the floor and crossed his arms over his chest. "Why is your stake a little-known secret?"

"That's complicated."

"And above my pay grade, probably."

Finally, she cracked a grin. What a stunner she was. He wondered if anyone had ever told her. Probably. Men tended to not have very good filters when it came to beautiful women. They just vented their spleens, sometimes into the realm of harassment. He didn't think Colleen would be particularly flattered by a whistle of appreciation. She was probably the kind of woman who'd make sure a man who tried it would never whistle again. Time to tread carefully. Business first, pleasure later… assuming he could manage either.

"Now, as I was saying earlier. I'm a candid woman. I believe in word conservation, so I'm not going to drag this out."

He put his hands up, palms-out. "You're firing me. I think that may be a record." He couldn't say he was surprised. He had been warned, after all.

Her jaw sagged a brief moment, then she closed her mouth and straightened her spine. She tamped a pile of papers on her desk into a tidy stack and met his gaze with her dark one, but now some of the hardness of it had worn off. She was obviously tired.

"I'm sure you're quite competent, but when we had to fire our last custodian, I was actually relieved, even if it put me in a pickle at the time."

"Relieved?"

Her head bobbed once.

The shrill bleating of her phone interrupted whatever was about to pass through those pursed lips, and she sighed as she picked up the handset. "Yes?"

She was quiet for a moment, and Alan catalogued the changes in her expression, trying to guess what the hapless fool on the other end must have been feeding her. Her face went from curiously interested to concerned, to annoyed, to flat-out angry in the end with her cheeks blazing red and eyes narrowed to slits. She said nothing, but her jaw clenched at the hinges.

Holding her tongue, but why?

If he were any other man who'd just been more or less fired, he would have excused himself to allow her some privacy with her call, but he wasn't any other man. Whatever was happening on that other end might be information critical to his developing plans. Maybe if he were lucky, she'd tell him what was happening, seeing as how he was out the door, anyway.

Finally, she spoke. "We haven't planted potatoes in that field in about five years, so where did they come from? I know we destroyed all of last year's tiny potatoes that we couldn't sell, so none of those went in this year's seed."

Her eyelids closed and shoulders sagged as she processed the rest of it.

"Are we going to grow any of salable size for this season?"

The response made her pound her fist on the desktop.

"Dammit. What next? No, don't answer that. I was being rhetorical. We'll have to keep that field cordoned off and ... wait, do we have any buffer space between those and the tomatoes, or are those screwed, too?"

Alan rubbed the scruff of his chin. Must have been a pest of some sort that got into the crops.

"Yeah, I'll come out there and take a look this afternoon. I've got something to take care of first."

She hung up without further pleasantries.

"Some sort of blight?" he asked before she could part her lips to pick up her previous line of discussion.

She tamped that stack of paper into order once more and shook her head. "Nematode infestation. More potatoes affected than not, it seems. At least half of the crop has dead roots, and a quarter more haven't flowered yet." She laughed, and it was a dry, crazed sound. It sounded almost like she expected this particular disaster, but it couldn't be that. "We've already got one field lying fallow because of last year's rot infestation. First time in ages we didn't have our own potato seeds. My Irish ancestors are rolling in their graves right now and probably mocking me from the great beyond."

"So, the new seeds were infected, too? Are you sure you got rid of the last ones?"

She quirked one dark eyebrow upward and crossed her arms over her chest. "Did I personally oversee the destruction of the last crop and treatment of the soil? Yes. There were no seeds left over. We're dealing with a different problem."

"Awful luck then."

"Yeah, especially considering we planted twice the potatoes we usually do this year so we could build our seed stores back up. We used to have these beautiful heirloom potatoes, and then—" She made an explosion sound and rolled her eyes. "Anyhow, I'll cut to the quick here, Alan. Split Acres is falling apart faster than I can salvage it. I'm constantly bailing water out of this boat, but eventually at the current rate, it's going to sink, and being the dutiful captain that I am, I'll likely go down with it."

"Why don't you sell it?"

Anger flashed in her eyes, but when she spoke, her voice was even. Modulated. She'd probably had a lot of practice at that. "You probably wouldn't understand."

Oh, she had no idea.

"Try me." He smoothed on what he hoped was an open expression and clasped his hands atop his lap.

She studied his face a moment, and somehow he managed not to grin at her. God, it was hard, not grinning at her like a besotted schoolboy, even given the dire situation she was in.

"For one thing, Alan, I've never been a quitter. There's potential here to unlock, and I seem to be the only person who can see it. I've got to clean up the mess my father made first. He was never really the brains of the business. That was Richard."

"Ah." Oh yes. He'd heard that story. Split Acres and Emerald Tea Farm had once been one big farm—WhitSand—owned by Richard Whitman and Colleen's father—Joe Sanders. Sam Whitman came along later to help on the marketing end.

Joe and Richard had a falling out about twenty years ago, and they separated WhitSand Farm's assets into the two neighboring ventures. Richard went organic and made the Whitmans' unique tea blends the core of their business. Joe clung to his traditional farming roots—the typical cash crops of the area grown with the commercial farming methods he'd grown up with on his family farm. Both farms prospered at first, but then the Whitmans' business boomed, while things on the other side of the fence sagged. One disaster after another befell the Sanderses, and Alan had already pieced together that in recent years they were barely eking by. So, no, Colleen didn't really have to explain.

"Second, I would never forgive myself if this farm goes under. There were a lot of people who invested in Daddy's scheme, and I don't want to pay them back with failure."

"Why would his failure be yours?" If things were really that bad, she could have walked away. Turned her back on the shame she perceived.

She rolled her ink pen between her palms and stared at him.

Okay. He got it. Sometimes the legacy of failure clung to a family's name longer than those of success. He'd always been on the winning team.

"You have ideas to turn this place around?" He suspected she was running dangerously low on words for the day, but he had to ask.

She set down the pen and spun it on the desktop. "Some. I suspect not too many people are going to like them, but I'll do what I must to pinch off the bleeding arteries around here."

"As in unnecessary staff."

"Seems the most obvious place to start."

"I understand your reluctance in this matter. I do, but might I make a proposition?"

Her lips quirked up at one corner in a devilish smirk as she leaned back in her inadequate chair.

A woman like her should have been on a throne.

She swiveled left, then right, studying him. "Where are you from, Alan?"

Should have known that was coming.

He swallowed and rethreaded his fingers so his right thumb overlaid the left. "Originally? South Africa."

"Wow. No wonder I couldn't place the accent. You're a long way from home. How'd you end up in the Skagit Valley, of all places?"

"Long story and circuitous journey."

That was putting it mildly.

She breathed a sigh through parted lips and swiveled in her chair some more.

The way she watched him, studied him, wasn't the habit of a woman who got a thrill from being cruel. This was a woman who knew her actions had consequences that directly affected the people around her. She had a heart in that chest, and if Alan's guess was right, someone had taken advantage of its warmth before. He swore right then and there he wouldn't do the same. He needed to tread carefully—get what he needed without leaving her cold.

"I'm sorry, but I can't afford you. As it is, I'm running on about fifty percent capacity with field hands. They've stuck it out for as long as they have only because of loyalty. They could have gone to the tea farm and earned a few more dollars per day than what I can give them, but I guess they stayed on for *auld lang syne*."

Probably not the only reason. Yeah, the staff feared Colleen, but it seemed to be a healthy fear. The kind of fear most people reserved for bosses with the opposite genitalia of her own. The fact she didn't have it was probably what made her so fearsome.

"I understand you're having some cash flow problems," he said, draping his forearms over his knees and leaning forward. "I've been around farms long enough to know some years are lean, and some are better."

"Oh yeah? Do much farming in South Africa?"

He cringed, but she didn't see it because she'd turned and was looking out the window behind her desk at the fields in the distance.

"Your farm equipment is in disrepair. Your outbuildings need attention. Pretty sure the electrical system in this building isn't up to code."

Now she spun, brow wrinkled, with a warning in her eyes.

He wasn't going to let her get it out. "I'm qualified. I'm licensed in this state as an electrician and I can fix anything with a motor without too much trouble. Have you heard the way your pick-up purrs lately?"

She had the decency to blush. "You tuned up my truck?"

He bobbed his shoulders casually. "Sounded horrible. I didn't do it to suck up to the boss." Lie. "That thing scared small children every time it blew past."

"It's just sensitive," she mumbled.

"It's a menace, and you know it. What I did is just a short-term fix. You're going to have to replace that thing soon."

She opened her mouth, but he cut her off once more. He hoped she didn't think it was a habit. "I know—the money. You should be okay for a couple of months, but beyond that … you should start making plans."

"Well, that's two months longer than I thought I had. Figured it'd dump me on the roadside any day now."

"Just give me a chance, Colleen. What choice do you have? Hire out for a mechanic for each thing around here that needs work as you have the funds? Let me take care of it. You won't regret it. Hold my pay for a month if it'll make you more comfortable."

Both eyebrows shot up. "You're either crazy or desperate."

Neither. Just hopeful.

"I think you'll find that I'll actually save you money in the long run."

And in a month, he could sell her on his value, which came with a lot more than a tool belt and electrician certification.

"You make a compelling case, Alan, and I'm tempted to say yes, but you've got to explain to me how you're going to subsist with no income. If you tell me savings, I'll probably cry. Only one of us should be that miserable, and it might as well be me."

So, she wasn't even paying herself. Now that was a damn shame. What must her quality of life be like with nothing in her budget for pleasure? He had a sudden compulsion to buy her dinner. Take her out dancing. Spoil her. But he had to start small so as not to arouse her suspicion. She'd be suspicious enough in due time.

He drummed his fingertips atop his thighs and turned his gaze toward the ceiling as if to consider her words. "I live pretty simply. I'm in a small apartment in town, and, yes, I have some savings from my last jobs."

Liar, liar, pants on fire, his younger sister Kimi might say.

He cleared his throat. "One month will not break me."

"Why are you so eager to work here for free? Shouldn't be that hard for a qualified electrician to land a job ... or even hang out a shingle on his own."

Well, there was the citizenship issue he'd been carefully skirting for a year, but she didn't need to know that.

"I love farm culture," he hedged. "It's a great thing to be a part of when it's working well."

A little huff escaped her lips and she pressed her hands to the desk edge and pushed her chair back. "Fine. A month. It's an unbeatable offer, and we've already established that I'm hard up." She stood. "Don't share that."

"Of course not." His cheeks twitched from the triumphant grin he was suppressing, but Colleen didn't seem to notice.

"Great. I've got to go deal with those potatoes, but um ... " She was halfway to the door before she turned back around and snapped her fingers. "Trial employment or not, I need your I-9 form on my desk in the morning."

Damn it.

"Certainly, Colleen," he said through clenched teeth.

She nodded and disappeared into the hall.

That went south faster than he expected. Short of acquiring a fake passport, his gig was up. But maybe if he kept her busy, she'd forget she asked. Once she learned his last name, she'd likely ship his ass out on the fastest thing running.

CHAPTER THREE

Colleen took another sip of her iced coffee and shuffled through the thick stack of records once more. Things just weren't adding up. Normally, farm disasters didn't sit with her for so long. They were par for the course around Split Acres, and since taking the operations helm, she'd developed a coping strategy of handling them and moving on. She couldn't put out other fires if she were still staring at the ash of the last one she extinguished, so she'd learned to compartmentalize.

But this potato issue just didn't smell right, figuratively speaking. There were no potatoes left after the last failed crop—no seeds to carry over. She'd overseen everything from the re-tilling of the fields to the application of the pesticides to contain the blight to that section of the farm. At the rate they were going, they would never be able to seek organic certification. There was always some new problem that required big guns to address it. The only thing they could claim as organic at that point were their apples, but even those were contentious because the border between the orchards and the fields was a bit narrow.

"You keep on thinking so hard, Colleen, and you're going to pop that blood vessel in your forehead." Pixie White slid a steaming hot blue plate special in front of her and laid a fork and knife at the side.

She managed a grin and set down her highlighter marker. Pixie had taught Colleen in grade school but quit not long after because the pay was better in waitressing.

The diner was on the other side of the county line, and although there were a number of very good, and reasonably affordable restaurants in Emerald Springs, since moving home Colleen hadn't had any particular desire to be spotted in any of them. She was like her mother that way.

If people saw her, they'd want to chat—ask her how things were going at the farm—and she'd have to do her usual obfuscating song and dance. She'd never been a liar, and lacked her father's grace in changing the subject.

Daddy could have a person discussing crop yields in one breath and the current Seahawks season in the next, and they wouldn't even realize they never got an answer to their question. He used that skill regularly in Olympia. Perhaps he should have been a lawyer rather than a farmer.

"Sorry, Pixie. Got a bit of a mystery on my hands, and it's probably going to cost me tens of thousands of dollars."

She shuddered even confessing it. The only reason the farm was in the black, and barely, was because Colleen was infusing money into it from her own accounts. Maybe she'd get lucky and have a child who'd become something stable and reasonable like a doctor and would finance her old-age nursing home stay, because the remnants of her retirement fund had gone kaput when one of the farm's irrigators croaked.

Daddy had always handled the finances by putting off paying one bill to pay a more urgent one, if necessary, and all that was culminating now with the farm having next to no credit. Having to buy nearly everything with cash upfront was shaping up to be one of the final nails in the farm's coffin. If only she could have leased that land to the Whitmans when Adam had solicited her for it again last month … that would have been cold, hard cash upfront, but she'd had to tell Adam no without even pretending to think about it.

Truth was, she'd broached the subject of trimming some of the land at the property border in a flat-out sale to the tea farm to her parents just days before Adam's first proposition. Daddy's response to the query had been some variation of "hell no" that Mom had suggested he never again utter in polite company.

"I'm not going to give them a damned inch of my land, Colleen. You'll have to figure something else out," he'd amended.

Colleen huffed and dug her fork into her green beans. Oh, she'd figure something out, all right. She was just spiteful enough that by the time she was done cleaning up Daddy's mess, she would make it so he'd never have to worry about making new ones.

Richard Whitman was retiring and handing the reins over to his eldest child, so maybe it was time for Daddy to do the same.

"That vein in your forehead is throbbing again, Colleen." Pixie returned with a slice of pie and a fresh iced coffee.

"I didn't order pie."

Pixie pushed her cat-eye glasses up her nose and shook her head. "Nope. He did." She crooked her thumb toward the lunch counter, and Colleen leaned back to spy Alan turned on his stool.

He smiled and waved.

She pushed an eyebrow upward and let her gaze flit down to the dessert so she could see what she was refusing before she sent it back.

Dammit.

Pixie's Blueberry Special. Her favorite and bonus points for it being cold. It wasn't going anywhere but her belly.

Pixie eased away from the table, and Colleen waved the man over.

"I've got a soft spot for blueberries and pie crusts made with real lard," she explained, bringing the tines of her fork down the pie side to nudge off a piece of the pastry.

He slipped into the other side of the booth and made a little drawing motion on one palm as if he were taking notes. "I'll remember that for later."

"Do I seem like the sort of woman who could be easily swayed by culinary blackmail?" She slipped the bite of pie between her lips and closed her eyes as the tart fruit hit all the right notes on her tongue. Oh yes. Yes she was *exactly* that sort of woman. No man had ever bought her pie before, though, that she could remember.

"If you were, it'd make my life a lot easier. What are you doing way out here?"

Pixie returned yet again, set down a huge wedge of chocolate cake in front of him, and topped off the coffee cup he'd brought over from the counter.

Colleen's mouth watered at the site of that chocolate decadence. Three layers of cake she knew would be just the right combination of moist and bready, sandwiched between thick slabs of fudge frosting. Dear God, that particular dessert would sit on her hips and thighs for weeks, because once she started with one slice, she'd tell Pixie to box up the rest of the cake in the display "for later." If Colleen could go to bed without polishing off half the damn thing, she deserved a medal.

Alan must have noticed her eyeing his plate because he nudged it toward her. "Would you like some?"

She swallowed, and tore her eyes away from the sinful thing, back to the real food—the protein and starch and vegetables—in front of her. She stuffed her mouth with meatloaf and shook her head vigorously.

He grinned, and it wasn't the kind of smarmy smile she'd grown to expect from men of late. He seemed genuinely amused by her.

Odd. Someone thought scary, cold Colleen was funny?

"Don't like chocolate?"

She took a long sip of her iced coffee and pointed to the glass. "If it weren't for that pie, this would have been all the sugar I allowed myself for the day. Me and chocolate were BFFs and decided our relationship had become too intense. We're on a breather."

He laughed. "You'd like my little sister, I think. She puts chocolate up on a pedestal that's borderline sacrilegious. Our father has often wondered if she should seek treatment for it."

"Hey, chocolate's a girl's best friend. It's sweet, sometimes a little nutty—but that's okay—and it doesn't talk back." She winked at him with that last bit, and his smile broadened in return.

When her breath hitched, she silently cursed her traitorous lungs and turned her gaze back to her meal.

Was she flirting? *No.* Never with staff, even if the particular employee in front of her made her want to keep talking for some damn reason. He just seemed so novel and exceptional compared to the Emerald Springs ordinary, and no man had pinged her radar screen so boldly since she'd moved home. It was almost as if she'd lost the requisite programming that made women sit up and pay attention when men crossed their paths, but he seemed to have rebooted her libido, and her eyes were working just fine.

She knew, though, that any misstep would set the wrong impression, not just with Alan, but for any staff who happened to witness one of her rare displays of humanity, such that it was.

"You didn't answer my question. What are you doing dining way out here alone?"

No one had ever asked before. Pixie could guess, so Colleen had never bothered making up a lie. Should she tell him the truth?

She set down her fork and tented her fingers over her dinner, staring at him.

He stared right back, his gaze clear and blue as the summer sky and a startling contrast to his tanned skin. He must have spent hours outdoors.

She broke her stare first and looked down at her own pale hands. She couldn't keep a tan anymore. Most of the light she got was from the fluorescent bulbs over her desk and through the windows of her truck when she was out running errands. She'd become a desk jockey in the prime of her life.

That was unexpected.

She cleared her throat and stared at the rich, dark gravy on her meatloaf. "I sometimes come out here knowing no one will see me, and that I won't have to talk."

When she turned her gaze back up to him, his smile had waned a bit.

"And here I am intruding on what's probably a rare moment of solitude."

She bobbed her shoulders. Pity, she didn't want. Pity got in the way of attraction, and for once she wanted to be found attractive, in spite of how she knew she looked at the moment. "Solitude, I get plenty of. What are you doing out here?"

"Followed you." He was so matter-of-fact in his tone, she waited for him to recant.

He didn't. He just pulled his cake closer and picked up his fork. "You followed me? Why?"

"Wanted to make sure nothing fell off your truck."

"You said my truck would be fine for a while."

"Maybe I was being overly optimistic."

Was he joking? She dropped her hands into her lap and studied his serious countenance as he ate bite after bite of that chocolate killer.

He was bluffing. Had to be. She should have known that trick herself, because hadn't she used it enough?

"Wait. You must have been here before me. You were already done eating when my food came."

"I like you, Colleen. You're smart."

Her belly fluttered like she was some fifth-grader with a crush on a seventh-grader. As far as pick-up lines went, if that even counted, it was a simple one, but effective. He seemed to be reading her like a picture book. She cleared her throat and shifted her attention to her iced coffee glass. "I like being liked, I guess, but really, why are you here?" She ripped open a pair of sugar packets.

He wrapped a large hand around the ceramic mug in front of him and brought it to his lips. After a long draught, he said, "This is one of the first places I ate at when I came into the area. I come out here every now and then for the cake."

"What, you haven't fallen head-over-heels for one of the many Whitman-owned establishments like everyone else in town?" There was an edge to her voice he didn't deserve, but the Whitmans were so entrenched in everything in the valley that it seemed nothing Split Acres ever did would be good enough. They would always be in second place ... assuming Emerald Tea Farm didn't take that, too, along with third and honorable mention.

Their tea was everywhere. They had a restaurant, a resort, and now even a bakery with Zoe Miller preparing to marry into the clan.

What did Split Acres have? A lot of fallow fields, a bunch of apples and pears, some lazy bees, and three half-constructed greenhouses that if they ever got finished, the farm might actually turn around a bit. Colleen had big plans for those greenhouses.

His expression went serious again as he brought the fork down into a particularly large glut of fudge frosting.

She whimpered at it.

"I like keeping my mind open," he said finally.

"Hmm."

She finished her blue plate special right as Pixie returned to top off Alan's coffee and clear away some of the plates.

Colleen pulled her pie close and said in a low, guilty voice to Pixie, "Can you bring me the rest of that cake? To go? For the weekend, you know." She'd have to budget her food purchases for the rest of the week, but it'd be worth it. She was pretty sure chocolate cake covered most of the major food and mineral groups, anyway.

Pixie murmured an "mm-hmm" and strode to the kitchen.

"So, tell me," Colleen said, cutting her pie slice into manageable chunks. "How does one land in Emerald Springs via South Africa?"

She didn't really expect him to answer. After all, he hadn't earlier when she'd asked. He'd danced around the question, so she was stunned when he said, "I left home at twenty-two wanting to see the world, so I signed on to work on a cruise ship."

"A cruise ship?" She dropped her chin and cocked one eyebrow up, hoping to convey her disbelief. The image that popped into her head was of the handsome handyman in little white shorts and a captain's hat serving drinks to inebriated MILFs.

Heat crept up her neck. She just bet he had great legs inside those weathered blue jeans.

"Yes. Wanted to improve my English, and that was a good way to do it."

"What's your first language?"

"That would be a tie between Afrikaans and French with English coming when I started my schooling. My mother was from France and my father is descended from Huguenots. Where I grew up was so isolated that he never bothered learning English until he needed it to read the major newspapers. That was before the internet and instant translation, you know? When I left home, I was fluent in English but only on paper."

"Wow. What language do you dream in?"

His eyes narrowed with amusement and he leaned back against the padded booth, chewing his bottom lip.

It was a sight far too sensual for daylight—one that made her feel like a voyeur for watching, but she couldn't stop looking. Every movement the man made seemed like a tiny sin.

After a moment, thankfully, he broke the trance and said, "I don't know. I guess I've never paid much attention and focused more on pictures than sound. Next time I have a dream, I'll let you know."

What did handymen dream about?

She worked some pie around on her tongue, barely tasting it, and swallowed. "Don't take this the wrong way 'cause there are a lot of stereotypes in play that I'm probably drawing on here, but of all places, why did your mother go from France to South Africa?"

"Mail-order bride," he said without losing a beat.

His voice was so flat she didn't know if she should laugh or scoff, so she just stared.

He grinned, and it reached the corners of his eyes.

"Damn you." He'd used another one of her conversational tactics, and if people felt nearly as disarmed as she did at the moment, no wonder they avoided her.

He chuckled and licked the last bit of fudge off the back of his fork.

She groaned inwardly, wishing she were fudge. God, what was *wrong* with her? She must have been overworked, because she never succumbed to distractions this way, masculine or otherwise.

"I think that like me, Mother experienced a bit of wanderlust in her youth. South Africa hadn't been her destination, but it ended up being her landing pad."

"I see. And is Washington State your landing pad or are you still wandering, Alan?"

He rotated his coffee mug between his palms and looked out the window to his right. "I'd like to stay still a while."

"Is that dependent on your job at my farm?"

"Perhaps it is."

The tentative smile she'd been wearing drew in. She didn't want to be responsible for anyone's long-term plans falling apart, but people shouldn't make bets on Split Acres. In a year, at the current rate, she was unsure if it'd still exist.

When her phone buzzed in her pocket, she snaked her hand inside the fabric, drew it out, and activated the call before she even had the device at her ear. "This is Colleen."

Alan turned his face from the window and watched her wearing an expression of curiosity as Pixie returned with a large pastry box and the check.

"Hey, love, it's Greg. Sorry to catch you outside the office, but I wanted to let you know I was going to be in the area tomorrow."

She perked up and swapped the phone to her other ear. An ally in town? That was exactly the sort of distraction she needed. Perhaps a visit from Greg would help ease this odd feeling of delirium brought on by Alan's arrival. She needed familiarity. She could control what was familiar.

She reached for the check, but it wasn't there. Neither was Alan's.

Pixie had made another circuit and must have picked it up without waiting for her card. She'd have to come back.

"Tomorrow?" Colleen asked, turning her attention back to the phone. "What are you doing up here?"

"We're shooting some catalog images at some place near you … uh, what is it? Hold on a sec."

She put her hand over the mouthpiece and furrowed her brow at Alan. "Where's the check?"

Pixie returned at exactly that moment with a signature slip and a card he quickly tucked into his pocket.

He was fast, but not fast enough to hide the platinum-colored glint.

Platinum? Not even her Split Acres corporate card had been platinum before it had been canceled. Maybe he just had a designer card or something. Wasn't unheard of.

"Yeah, Emerald Paradise Resort," Greg said. "Place looked gorgeous in all the literature. Hoping to get some great, authentic shots of our models in the new waterproof hoodies."

Of all the places they could have chosen, of course it had to be a Whitman-owned establishment. She felt as though her old world and new one were intersecting, and not in a good way.

"Hope it rains on you," she said drily. "It'd make for some good, authentic misery."

"*Yeowtch*. What bee flew up your skirt?"

She closed her eyes and took a deep, steadying breath before responding. Greg didn't deserve the snark. No one did, really, except maybe Daddy, and he wasn't at the farm enough to receive his due. "I'm sorry. It's been a long day."

"I know what that's like. Listen, I'll stop by with those palettes and fabric swatches for the boots and rain hats at around ten. Where are you going to be then?"

"Around ten, huh? Either in the orchards checking the new grafts, the flower fields, marking off bulb types, or in my office at the corporate building. Can't miss it. I'll tell my secretary to expect you."

"Cool deal. See you in the morning, love."

"Yeah."

Greg hung up.

She turned her attention to Alan and found him scooping her cake box into his arms.

He stood and bobbed his head toward the exit. "I hope you don't mind if I follow you home. I won't be able to sleep thinking about that truck."

She swept her arm toward the door and bowed sarcastically. That short phone call had done wonders to douse her libido, and she was almost back to even keel because of it. Back in control. "Be my guest."

He could trail her home all right, but he didn't need to be so damned friendly with her cake.

CHAPTER FOUR

"You may as well come in and set the cake down since you've come this far." Colleen held the screen door open wide with her foot, and gestured toward the rear of the house.

He stepped into the spartan living room and took in the ambience, what little there was. Aside from a sofa, a pair of end tables, a coffee table topped with a smattering of papers, and a bleached-out braided rug, there wasn't much to see. He hadn't known what to expect from an inscrutable woman like her, but somehow the lack of personality in the place seemed tragic.

She let the door snap shut and eased around him, close enough to make the hair on his forearms stand on end but not quite touching.

Tease.

She turned and stuffed her hands into her pockets, eyeing him. "I know what you're thinking. I never got around to decorating because I didn't think I'd be here this long. Figured I would have moved into town, but free is a lot more appealing than fashionable at the moment. All of my stuff is in storage. I haven't had the heart to move it in here, but I guess I will sooner than later."

He pulled free of her dark, mesmerizing stare to take in the plain beige walls and dull wood floors. "It's not that bad," he lied.

"Right." She nodded sarcastically. "It's easier not to argue. Kitchen's this way." She leaned her head toward the hallway.

"Onward, then."

She maneuvered through stacks of outdoor gear catalogs, almanacs, and assorted footwear, and he followed close on her heels. In the kitchen doorway, she paused, and smacked the wall where the light switch must have been.

Nothing happened.

She murmured a surprisingly unfeminine oath under her breath and toggled the switch again. She grunted and pounded her fist on the drywall.

"You want me to change the bulb for you?"

"It's not the bulb. I should know. I've changed it three times this week, though by now I should really know better. I keep holding out hope that maybe the *right* bulb will come along and make the fixture want to clean up its act."

He laughed.

"Sometimes the light works, sometimes it doesn't. At least it didn't crackle this time."

"*Shit*, Colleen," Alan quickly shifted the weight of the heavy cake to one arm and used his free hand to tap down the switch. "That's what folks in the trade call a *fire hazard*. Let's just leave it off, okay? I'll take a look at it tomorrow in the daylight. If the wiring in here is anything like the rest of the farm, I'll likely be spending half the day in your attic yanking it all out. I'd bet your outlets aren't grounded, either."

She did a shifty sideways look that confirmed such.

"I'll start tomorrow. Is it just this back half of the house that's intermittent at the moment? That would be my priority."

She sighed. "No. As much as the idea of reliable overhead lighting really does it for me, the stuff out there," she crooked her thumb toward the window behind her and indicated the greater farm beyond, "needs more attention right now. I'm used to doing things in the dark."

She moved from the hallway into the kitchen, tossing a glance at him over her shoulder. The way her lips teased up at the corners suggested her words had a deeper meaning than he'd initially parsed.

"And taking cold showers?" he asked, and dragged his right sleeve across his forehead. It had suddenly gotten very warm in

Colleen's kitchen, and he was fairly sure they hadn't sparked an electrical fire in her walls.

She turned and he could see her grin in the light from the refrigerator she'd opened. There was a dare in her lovely features, and he'd never been the kind of man to refuse a challenge.

"Nope. Water heater has natural gas and all the big appliances are on their own switches. So, no shortage of steam here ... assuming I want it."

"I see." *So, that's the game we're playing.* He had a number of comebacks on the tongue that could either get him slapped, fired, or both. He squashed them and slid the cake onto the rough-hewn farm table.

She turned away and bent into the open refrigerator. If she thought she was hiding that shapely rear end inside those baggy black cargo pants, she was sorely mistaken. He ogled brazenly, because contrary to what the Split Acres staff said, it was unlikely she had eyes at the back of her head.

He liked his women with a little roundness, usually, but there was something nice about Colleen's fit curves, too. Athletic without being waifish or else too bulky. Long, lean muscle with a bit of padding for him to grab hold of.

He clenched his hands into fists at his sides and rolled his eyes toward the ceiling. *Focus.* He couldn't let this woman distract him when he was supposed to be trying to preoccupy *her*, and his plan hadn't been to do it with sex.

Now that it was on his mind, though ... *shit.* He wanted to know how she'd be—whether she'd be aggressive or wait for him to take the lead.

The refrigerator door snapped shut, and that sultry voice said with a laugh, "Does my wiring really bother you that much, Alan?" She tapped a light switch near the back door and the patio light came on, adding a bit more illumination to the room.

He lowered his gaze to find her smiling in the dim light, and her amusement settled into the creases at the outer corners of her eyes.

Wiring? What about the wiring?

Why did he follow her home again? His gaze trailed down to her hand—to elegant fingers wrapped around the neck of a plastic bottle—then up her torso to full breasts his stare may have lingered on for longer than necessary.

She cleared her throat, and he pulled his gaze to her face once more. Her lips pursed as she considered him, and she likely thought him daft, standing there staring as if he were waiting for silent commands from his mothership.

God, her lips. When she wasn't scowling at him and pressing them into an unfortunate tight line, they were fabulously lush. Pink.

She cleared her throat again, and he drew in a breath and strode toward the counter. With that light from the back, he could see now that the wallpaper behind the toaster oven was some mid-century olive, gold, and cream pattern of corn stalks and wheat. Garish.

Oh. The *farm.* That's why he'd followed her home. Not for Ms. Sanders personally. This was a business transaction, really, and she was merely an unexpected distraction. If he could wrangle her, then Joe Sanders should fall into line right behind her. She wasn't just going to hand the farm over to him because he asked nicely and handed her a fat check. This scenario required some finesse, and at the moment she was the one finessing *him.* That's why she was the boss, apparently.

"Yes, I guess they do," he said finally. "Listen, I have a proposition I—"

"Do you want a drink?" she interrupted, holding the bottle of what he now could see was cola. "You can have cola, rum, or some combination of the two."

"What are you having?"

Her shoulders drew upward and then fell. "Mostly rum. Helps me sleep. Quiets the niggling to-do list that churns in my head when I lie down."

"I'll have mostly cola, then. These roads are dark, and I want to be clear-headed."

Right. For the *roads*.

She lifted the cola bottle in salute. "You got it. I wish I could actually get drunk in the way some people do. I either fall asleep or end up on the cold tile of the bathroom floor, staring at the ceiling until I pass out because if I close my eyes, the swirling will make me throw up."

"Poor thing."

"I know. I can't even do that Irish bit right, huh? First the potatoes, now my booze intolerance. Got the translucent winter skin and unpredictable temper, though. Better watch out. Word on the street is that I scream and scratch."

Yeah, I'll make you scream, all right.

As she puttered around, pulling down glasses from the cabinets and rum from the sideboard, he shifted position to the doorway where the light was better and leaned against the frame. He racked his mind for any question that would send their conversation in a more professional direction. As it was, he was silently praying to whichever god would hear that a certain appendage of his stayed at ease instead of standing up to salute.

"So, what's your sport, Colleen?"

If she heard the strain in his voice, she didn't acknowledge it. Her fingers stilled over the rum cap and she turned her head toward him. "I'm sorry?"

"Do you play a sport? You seem to ... " *inspire all sorts of inappropriate carnal images.* "... have the bearing of an athlete." Legs that went on for days and sexy-as-hell hips. Farmers didn't look like that where he came from.

"Oh." She splashed a finger of rum into one glass and three into the other before replacing the cap. "Lacrosse. Field hockey." She laughed. "I guess I like playing with sticks. I'm pretty deadly."

Sticks. Heat surged into his belly and he rolled his tense shoulders back. "Really, lacrosse? We should toss the ball sometime. My brother and I used to play. Lacrosse isn't huge in South Africa like it is here, but it's catching on."

She laid her head a bit to the side and thrust a drink at him, scoffing. "Right. I'm out of practice. I could probably indulge you if I had the free time, but I wouldn't bet on me."

"Well, that's defeatist thinking." That was better. A bit of sports talk always seemed to turn the heat down. He followed her into the living room and took the seat she indicated.

She sat in the other sofa and crossed her rubber booted feet up atop the table. "It's not defeatist. It's realist. That's me. Ruthlessly real."

"I see." Given he was probably about to loose some of that ruthlessness onto himself, he was very interested in its bounds. How far would she go to have her way? What would he have to do to make her bend?

He sipped his drink and watched her stare through the screen door. She ran her free hand over her now messy bun.

What would all that hair look like let down? Would it reach her shoulders? Her breasts?

Before his gaze could finish its track down her torso, he closed his eyes and blew out a breath.

He couldn't do this. Not with her. This plan of his had already gone sideways. He'd hoped to go about this in a more businesslike fashion, once he'd set his mind to it. He saw a farm with a lot of potential, but no money. Here he was, a man with lots of money—well, sort of—and a good deal of farming knowledge. Split Acres should have been an easy enough acquisition, and one his family would have reveled in.

Most people bent when offered enough cash, regardless of what their principles were and how rigid their resolves.

He'd thought he'd come in and make nice with the Sanderses. Get them to trust him, and at the right time, introduce them to his big family back home. His father was itching to gain a foothold in the United States. He wanted to become a direct competitor to Emerald Tea and expand the Prevost offerings beyond rooibos and wine. And to own the land right next door to the big tea producer? Well, that would be a major coup.

But the more he thought about it, he didn't really want his family to buy Split Acres. The Prevosts had gotten where they were by being ruthless. They didn't care about burning bridges and hurting feelings, but Alan did. He wanted Split Acres for himself—something to build from the bottom up—and having Colleen there both complicated and improved his situation.

She might have been the key to the trust fund he hadn't given a shit about until now, but he had to engage her carefully. She wasn't some cold bitch playing CEO while Daddy was away. This wasn't a woman he could run roughshod over. She was a beautiful, intelligent, *funny* woman with a lot of problems ... him being one soon, if he went through with his plan.

He needed to convince her it was best if he took it off her hands.

When she set her empty glass onto the coffee table and stood, he did the same and followed her to the door.

"Love these starry nights." She looked up the long path toward the road, stretching her arms high over her head so her shirt crept up past her navel.

Seeing that creamy stretch of skin must have shorted some circuit in his brain, much like Colleen's kitchen lights because before he knew it, he'd stopped fretting about the farm again. One of his hands was on her waist, inching around to her spine, and then the other hand joined in so he pulled her front against his.

He realized what he did too late, but once he did he wouldn't let go. Didn't apologize. She felt nice. He'd known she would.

She rolled her eyes up to him and furrowed her forehead. She pressed her palms against his chest but didn't quite push. "Alan, what are you doing?"

"It was a reflex." There. One small truth to make up for all the lies.

"You have a cuddle reflex?"

"I guess you could call it that."

Her skin was so warm, so silky beneath his hands, he could hardly be expected not to sample it further. To memorize its feel. He grazed his fingertips up her spine and drew a shudder from her.

She liked his touch, but would she permit him to touch more? See more? She'd been teasing him all night. She had to have expected he'd stop talking soon and act.

His hands slipped up the back of her shirt, and her fingers wrapped around his wrists. She stared at him, her face a blank. She neither pushed, nor pulled.

After a moment, he recognized her tentativeness. She was lost without a roadmap for this sort of scenario. No compass to navigate the social niceties, if he could even call them that. She was his boss, sort of, and this was his first day on the job. If she were feeling anything at all similar to what he was, niceties didn't even come into play, just impulses. Base, carnal cravings that couldn't be suppressed no matter how many pitiful prayers he murmured.

The way he was feeling—half-crazed and skin-starved—couldn't be described in any stretch of the imagination as "nice."

What had Pixie said to her? That she was thinking too hard? Yes, he could see that now in her dark eyes as she assessed him.

He was dealing with enough mania himself that he certainly didn't want to add to hers, so he did what he did at the diner and distracted her. Instead of with pie, this time, he dipped his head and brushed his lips across hers.

He waited for a flinch. A jerk backward. A slap—*anything*.

None of those things came. Instead, she loosened her grip on his wrists.

When her eyes closed and her fingers glided around and tucked beneath the fabric of his shirt back, he leaned in again. This time, he tasted her lips in a slow circle before slipping his tongue between her parted lips.

She tasted of rum and soda. Of blueberries. Smelled like coffee and sweetly cloying shampoo. Felt warm and real and vulnerable.

She'd been jumbling his thoughts and motivations from the moment he'd watched her step over that dog, and no matter what he did until the day he died, he'd never be able to forget this moment and his odd mixed feelings of triumph and terror.

Perfect woman, wrong time.

Fuck.

His mind churned with thoughts of home and business and money and everything else all at once, so he hardly noticed when Colleen eased them away from the threshold and shut the inner wooden door.

They moved as a unit down the hall, still connected, still kissing, and entered a room that must have been the master suite.

He barely registered the backs of his legs hitting the mattress side, nor falling back onto it with Colleen on top of him.

It wasn't until she peeled her shirt over her head and whispered, "Don't tell anyone," that lucidity slammed into him like a rampaging rhinoceros.

She wanted him, too, and his mind reeled at the prospect of her consent.

This thing he was doing was so wrong, but this proximity to her—this joining—felt so right. Under different circumstances, he would have never gotten close. Never asked her out because she was like an artifact in a glass case. Untouchable.

Once this mission had turned into a business prospect, he'd been able to lump the woman in with the farm and think of them as one unit. But then he *saw* her.

"Off," she said, pulling at the front of his shirt.

"Yes." He sat up, carefully so as not to dislodge her from his lap, and shed his shirt.

Her lips pressed into the crook of his neck and deposited hot kisses downward to his pecs, his navel, his waistband. She slipped off the edge of the bed and onto her knees on the floor beside it.

"Off," she said again, breathily, now tugging his belt buckle unfastened. Quick fingers worked his button free and eased his fly to the base.

"Of course." He raised his rear off the bed and let her shimmy his jeans down his legs. They stopped at the tops of his boots, but she wasn't put off by the obstacle for long. She pulled his boots at the heels, easily dislodging them, and pushed them away from the bedside along with his jeans.

He leaned back onto his elbows, watching her stand and heel off her own footwear and wishing he was bold enough to turn on that lamp on the bedside table. She'd said she was used to doing things in the dark, but he wanted to see. What he could see of her in the faint light was breathtaking, but he would have liked to memorize every freckle, every scar. Everything that made her Colleen and not some anonymous warm body.

"You really are practical, aren't you?" he asked when she stepped out of her pants and dropped her underwear with no further teasing.

"Are you complaining?" She reached back and unfastened her bra with one swipe of her hand.

"Absolutely not. I like it." He joined her in nudity, quickly shedding his boxer briefs as she worked her bra straps down her arms.

Then they both stilled in the dark, eyeing what they could of each other and waiting for some cue to engage.

He started the dance, so he figured it was up to him to lead it.

He pulled her into the open vee of his legs and skimmed his hands down her back, kneading the small of it before cupping her rear. He pressed his face against her belly and kissed, laved at her navel until she shuddered, then pulled her on down top of him as he leaned back.

She didn't need advice or suggestion. She just eased back until her warm apex met his arousal, and then she seated herself on him slowly.

Her face tilted toward the ceiling and she blew out a long breath once he was in as far as he could go. "It's been a while," she whispered, and it wasn't the whisper of a teasing siren. It was the soft voice of a woman unsure of herself.

He laced his fingers through hers as she found her rhythm. "You'll have to excuse me for not being disappointed."

And there was nothing disappointing about what she was doing, and maybe he was a bit frightened by it. The way her hands shook atop his jarred him, made him want to forget about himself temporarily and make sure her needs were met. It seemed like such a small favor.

He moved her hands so they pressed against his chest and nudged the loose swaths of hair in her face behind her ears. He wished he could see her face more clearly, to see if this was *enough* for her, but what little light there was, was at her back. Normally, he would have taken his time and explored every inch of her skin, but nothing he'd done with the woman so far had gone according to plan.

Slipping his hand behind her neck, he pulled her down and found her lips.

Her body tensed at first, but as her free hand skimmed down her spine, she parted her lips and fell into a slow rhythm atop him.

Her toes curled against his calves and her breath shuddered, and he held her tighter, crushing her soft breasts against him.

His body wanted him to thrust—to claim her the way a spirited woman needed to be claimed—but her shaking hands betrayed her control. She may have needed someone else to take the lead on occasion, but right now, he wanted her to set the pace. To trust that he wouldn't demand more than she was capable of giving, at least in the bedroom.

"Are … are you close?" she whispered as her knees tightened at his hips.

"Were you waiting for me?"

"Yes."

Fuck. "Go. Please, go."

And when she did, it took everything he had to hold back his own orgasm. Her body seemed to need the release so badly, and he was glad to give it to her, but he wasn't ready for his own.

He loosened her hair so it fell onto his face, kissed her chin, down her neck, and across her shoulders until she sighed. Then he rolled her onto her back and wrapped her legs around his waist.

"Yes?"

"Yes," she whispered back, already reaching for him.

She seemed to trust he wouldn't push her past her limits.

All he could hope was that she wouldn't regret it, in spite of what may come.

CHAPTER FIVE

Colleen stretched beneath her sheets, grinning at the fabulous night of sleep she'd had. The last time she'd slept so well was when she was working at Markson and had to fly into Maine for a couple of days of meetings. She hadn't *meant* to sleep through that important breakfast, but the night before had been a late one, and critical to upcoming product development.

"Wait." She forced her eyes open and rubbed them. The room was too bright. What time was it? And why hadn't Alan woke her before he left?

She sat up and squinted at her alarm clock.

"Damn it."

Throwing the covers back, she leapt from the bed and hurtled herself into the bathroom.

Already ten. Greg must have thought she'd flaked … or maybe he'd thought she got caught up in farm business. Hopefully, he wasn't walking around the farm and itemizing its disrepair.

She barely registered all the motions she went through—washing her hair and shaving her legs—as she was fuming too hard, thinking too much about the night that had just transpired and what it meant. All she knew was that somehow she transformed into a greater state of cleanliness and found herself in front of the sink, wrapped in a towel, with hair dripping wet.

Tying her long hair into a tight bun, she pondered the protocols for her particular situation. She'd not only slept with an employee whose last name she didn't know, but someone she wasn't in a committed relationship with. She hadn't been kidding when she said it'd been a while. The last time she'd warmed anyone's sheets had been about three years ago—before she'd moved home and made a mess of her formerly well-regimented life.

That time, she'd thought she was with the man who'd be her "forever" and "always," but he'd turned out to only be good for "right now," much like the one before him. With a history like that, Colleen couldn't help but take the snubbings personally.

Nudging one final bobby pin into her hair, she sighed and left the comfortably steamy bathroom.

She dressed in her favorite black boatneck shirt and black jeans without bothering with the lights, and padded to the kitchen with socks in hand. Unrolling the tubes onto her feet, she eyed the cake box with a bit of malevolence.

He'd paid for that cake. For her dinner. He was living on "savings," he'd said. Right. More likely, he had a sugar momma waiting in the wings, paying the bills each month for that platinum card he'd tried to hide away.

She'd need to take a closer look at his paperwork—his employment history. See where he really came from and figure out what kind of trouble he'd brought along with him.

She had enough trouble for two people already with all the tension between Split Acres and Emerald Tea, and she sure as hell didn't want to add anything new to the brew.

Grabbing her keys from the rack near the back door, she scanned the tidy row of rain boots in the mudroom and settled on the dark gray ones with black clouds. They fit her mood.

She was halfway to her truck when she snapped her fingers and backtracked to the house. The door lock turned with a peculiar ease, but she pushed back thoughts of that for the moment, and stomped through the house to the kitchen.

She grabbed the cake and tucked it under her left arm, storming back through the living room once more only to pause at the front door.

Her bleary eyes focused on the wall to the right where the switches controlling the porch light and living room lamps had been mounted. There'd always been a gap between the bottom of the switch plate and the actual hole in the wall where the wiring came up. The original antique plate had broken shortly before Colleen moved in, and her father had replaced it with whatever he could find. There'd been nothing to do for it because the panel of drywall needed replacing. Naturally, they hadn't bothered because the house needed rewiring.

Apparently, some industrious little South African worker bee took it upon himself to remove the switch plate and tidy the rectangular hole in the wall. The exposed wires had been clamped and dangled outside the drywall. A sticky note beside it read: "Killed the power in here. Will fix today. Sorry about the ceiling. Needed to work in attic while it was cool."

Her eyes tracked upward, and she swallowed hard, not knowing what to expect when her gaze hit the ceiling.

Four holes in square configuration ruined her formerly intact ceiling.

Casting her gaze back to the door, she seethed. She'd slept through that? Through six-inch diameter *holes* being cut through her ceiling? Slept through an obvious repair of the front door that had been sticking so long she had forgotten that wasn't the way doors were supposed to work?

"The nerve."

This was her space, and if she wanted to live in a dark, decrepit cave, then she'd live in a flippin' cave.

She shifted the cake to her other arm and shouldered the door open. She slammed it shut and strode to her truck: a woman on a mission of destruction.

Alan … what was his last name? Well, whatever it was, he was through. He'd crossed a line, and though Colleen couldn't specifically name which one, she knew it was a broad one.

She drove up the path in a rage, grinding her teeth as the operations building loomed closer. Once parked in her usual space at the immediate left of the doors, she marched into the reception area, cake in tow, and dropped the damned thing on the refreshment counter.

Kate raised an eyebrow but was smart enough not to query.

"That's chocolate cake," Colleen said, pointing at the pastel box. "Help yourself."

"Okay ... " Kate nudged the morning's courier deliveries toward her desk corner and then eased her rolling chair back. "I will." She stood, keys in hand, and walked to the metal cabinet near the windows. She unlocked it, plucked out a stack of small paper plates, forks, and a spatula, and re-locked the cabinet.

She set it all on the table and freed the cake from its boxy prison. "Hey there, precious. Come to Momma." She handed Colleen a large slice, cut one for herself, and stuck forks in both. "Now, you know I like free cake as much as anyone, but what's the occasion?"

"Firing party. Can you find Alan for me? Let me know where he is?"

Colleen carried her cake, keys, and mail down the hall, stepped over her father's dog, Arfer, and closed herself into her office.

Briefly, she shuffled through the envelopes, and found the one she'd nearly forgotten was coming.

With renewed energy, she sprang to her feet and pressed the envelope beneath her arm. The cake could wait. She needed to get into town and deposit that check before noon, or the farm vehicles would be going without diesel fuel for a while.

She pulled her door open only to bump chests with the exact person she didn't want to see at the moment.

Alan nudged her back across the threshold and shut the door. His grip on her upper arm was proprietary, and it confused her for a moment.

"You wanted to see me? Fortunately, I was nearby. Just got back from town."

Breathe, stupid.

She swallowed and tore her gaze from his intense blue one. She'd recognize those eyes anywhere, and now knew they were just as bewitching in the dark. He didn't close his eyes when he made love.

Hail Mary, full of grace …

She stuffed her shaking hands into her pockets. "Yes. Have a seat." She nodded toward the chairs, but he didn't budge. She shrugged and mumbled, "Suit yourself," and walked toward the desk herself.

He followed, but when she sat, he stood in front of the desk, crossing his arms over his chest.

"So … " she began. Keeping eye contact with the man held a challenge she was unfamiliar with.

Oh God. I had sex with him. Her cheeks burned hot, and she fixed her gaze on the paperwork piling up on her desk.

Huh. That's new. She drew a stack of forms she hadn't seen before closer and eyed them.

"I assumed that paperwork was why you wanted to see me."

"Actually, I just made it into the office, thanks a lot, so it wasn't. *Shh.* I'm reading." She studied the I-9 form and the supplementary photocopies Kate must have run. Well, he was legal after all. At least, superficially.

Vaguely, she registered him shifting his weight in front of the desk as she flipped through the rest. His certifications, a copy of his lease, his résumé …

"Um … what's all this for?" Now she could meet his gaze with impunity. All she needed was to put her mind back on work. Hard work—that's how she managed to get through high school with her virginity intact despite raging hormones and no dearth of local eye candy. Studying and tough sports requiring big sticks had done the trick.

His forehead furrowed, and he took that seat she'd offered now. "Kate figured it out when she ran the copies. I figured you would, too."

"I haven't had coffee yet. What am I missing here?"

"Perhaps you should take a closer look at my last name."

She crooked an eyebrow up at him, and his expression was now a blank mask.

"Okay." She flipped back to the topmost page—the I-9—and read it again. "Prevost."

A slow nod.

Still, the significance eluded her.

"Does the name not strike you as familiar, Colleen?"

She raised her shoulders briefly and let them fall. "Sorry."

He blew out a sputtering breath through his lips, stood, and eased around her desk. He hovered behind her, leaning down and reaching for her computer mouse.

She breathed through her mouth, refusing to tease herself with his scent, especially now that she knew what his skin tasted like.

When the password prompt activated, she typed in the memorized string of characters and navigated to the browser she assumed he needed.

He typed in a web address ending ".co.za," and a slick flash-animated site loaded on her monitor.

The realization made her feel very cold all of a sudden, even with Alan's close proximity. He was so near; in fact, his warm breath tickled her neck, which was still moist from her dripping hair. That warmth had made her squirm in his embrace the previous night.

God. She smacked a palm against her forehead. "You're ... one of *those* Prevosts?"

"I am." He didn't hesitate one second. "I suppose you know the name now."

"Well, yes. Who wouldn't know the name of the Whitmans' biggest international competitor? Didn't realize you had operatives in the United States now."

"It's not like that."

"So, how is it? You're obviously a little overqualified to be tinkering with doorknobs on my farm, so if you're not in Emerald Springs to spy on the Whitmans for your family's conglomeration, then why are you here?"

He eased away, the prickling hairs on her neck smoothed, and she was able to breathe a little easier. She squared her shoulders and put as much heat into her gaze as she could by the time he'd walked around to the front of her desk.

He took a seat and leaned in with his elbows propped atop his thighs, staring right back at her.

"Well? I mean, it makes good sense now that you wouldn't really need the month's pay. You probably have more in your rainy day fund than what would be in any check I issue you."

Which reminded her, she had a check to cash. She stood.

"Please wait." He put his hands up, palms out, in a calming gesture that actually had the opposite effect on her.

Was this guy kidding her? Making her out to be some kind of joke? Did he think he was going to make her scream half the night like a woman possessed then drop this bomb on her like everything was honky dory? And make a mess of her ceiling, to boot?

"Look, *Mr. Prevost*, I need to go deposit a check to keep my farm running a little while longer. Then I need to go do some freelance work to make up for that check I had to beg for. So, you'll have to excuse me if I'm a bit crusty. I'm sure you know how to find your way to the door."

He beat her to the exit and blocked it with his body. That tall, muscular body she'd wrapped her legs around that second time they'd had sex when she proved she really did scream and scratch.

God. She took a step back and pretended to be very interested in the John Deere calendar pegged beside the door.

"You need to listen. I can help you."

"Help me? How? By screwing me senseless and leaving a fun configuration of holes in my living room ceiling? I never liked playing connect the dots as a kid. Still don't."

"Holes in your kitchen, too. Guess you didn't notice. And let's leave the sex out of it because although it was wonderful, it's really irrelevant to our current discussion."

"Is it?" She met his gaze again, feeling a bit more in control now. "You don't think, even a little bit," she narrowed her eyes and held her clamped right thumb and forefinger in front his face, showing him just how *little* she meant, "that I would find you getting into my bed the night before you dropped this kind of bomb on me to be even the slightest bit suspicious? I mean, come on, Alan. I've known you a day. Is this supposed to be some kind of fatal attraction? Ensnare me, work your way close? To what end?"

"Yes, I wanted to get close, but will you let me tell you how I can help you?"

"How you can help *me*? You can help me by getting off my farm and pretending we never met."

Any other man would have reddened or blanched. Perhaps even squared his shoulders indignantly. This one had the nerve to push an eyebrow up at her.

"Will you *listen*? I can save your farm, Colleen. I can give you the money to pay off the bills. Get your staff back. Turn this place around."

"And why would you do that? Hmm? So the farm's in good shape for when your family is ready to come and a pluck it up for their conglomeration? That'd be a real feather in your cap, right? Right next door to your biggest competitor. You know, that actually makes some of the weird stuff going on around here lately make sense."

He had gall to furrow his forehead as if he didn't know. "What?"

She tried to open the door behind him, but he put his body in front of the knob.

Sighing, she smoothed a hand over her hair. *Better get that coffee, now.*

Giving up on exiting, she strode to the credenza and loosened the decanter from the machine. "All the suspicious sabotage attempts going on over at the tea farm. I know they suspect us, given the way Daddy and Richard have been sniping at each other for years. But what good would it do us to take them down a peg or two? We're not exactly competitors at this point, and I'm not the kind of woman who's so prideful she gets off on seeing others fail." She filled the decanter in the little adjoining washroom and returned to the machine.

"What about your father?"

"Yeah, well, I suppose he'd make a good suspect given the acrimony between him and Richard, but he's just an easy target. He hasn't even been here most of the past month … except to hire you."

She rolled her eyes, but he couldn't see it with her back turned.

"So you'll have to excuse me for being suspicious. Right now, to me, it makes more sense that you'd be behind some of the screwball Whitman happenings than anyone on this farm."

"You're wrong, but if you think that, I imagine others will, too, especially with what I'm about to propose."

She placed a filter in the coffeemaker and scooped in eight tablespoons of rich Colombian roast. "Lay it on me. I could use a laugh."

"Marry me, Colleen."

She dropped the scoop.

Laughing wasn't the visceral reaction her body found appropriate for the scenario. Her forceful gasp that gave way to coughing was far more suitable—and realistic.

He rubbed one of those large hands up and down her back until the coughing eased up.

"You're nuts," she said, wheezing.

"I'm serious," he said. "Can we sit? Finish with your coffee, of course, but I think you'll find what I have to offer will make that check you're rushing out to deposit look like a drop in the proverbial bucket."

She just bet it would, but why would he do such a thing?

The least she could do was listen. She'd always been credited with being an innovative thinker and a careful risk-taker. She'd listen to what he had to offer because maybe it'd be her ticket to finally edge her father out of the job at which he'd failed so spectacularly. This could be her means to repairing that hole in the collective family pride. And maybe she feared if she didn't listen, her farm would be the next one beset with a host of mysterious problems.

Her phone rang and she hit the speaker button without breaking her gaze with Alan. "Yeah, Kate?"

"Greg Quinton on line three. He wants to know if you're in the office. Said he couldn't reach your cell phone."

"Uh." Her eyes trailed down Alan's torso to the tanned fingers drumming his thighs. Talented fingers that had pushed her over the edge screaming twice. The man didn't just tinker. He'd gotten under her hood and made her purr.

Ugh.

She pressed her hand behind her neck and rubbed the knot out. "Kate, tell Greg I'll call him back. Something came up."

There was a long silence from Kate, and then she asked, "Personnel problem?"

"Yes."

"Want me to call the deputy?"

Colleen looked up to see Alan grin.

Ass.

"No. I can handle it, as always. Just deal with Greg."

"You got it."

The phone line buzzed with Kate's disconnection, and Alan tented his fingers. Before she could screw her head on straight, he said, "You should know my family is aware of the state of your farm. I'm the one who told them."

CHAPTER SIX

Colleen's dark eyes were intense behind the rim of her oversized mug. They seemed to bore through him, daring him to misspeak, although Alan suspected nothing he said at this point would go over well.

He'd made a mess of things, shouldn't have gotten entangled in emotions or her sheets, but Colleen Sanders was an extraordinary woman, regardless of what he had in mind for her farm. He didn't regret last night. Never would. Hell, if anything, he'd like to repeat it.

Get on with it.

"I know you distrust me. Yes, my family is aware of the state of your farm because I told them about it somewhat obliquely. I had a discussion with my brother several weeks ago and we went over a variety of things, including the local farms here. Mostly, we were discussing the tea farm, and I happened to mention Split Acres being the neighbor. Bit of a shark, my brother. He put two and two together. Did some research. Knows your farm has a lot of big bills coming due."

He tried not to let the red flush of her cheeks undo him, but recognizing that hint of emotion and not doing something to mitigate it in some way made him feel cruel. Still, he pressed on. He needed to get it all out before she cut him short. Knowing Colleen just a little, he knew there wouldn't be a second chance.

"Really, you have two choices. I can loan you a bit of money to patch some things here and there, but you don't need patches at this point. You need a full overhaul of this operation, and you know now I'm qualified to make that assessment. Or my family will wait until you fail and pick up the pieces for a song ... or the Whitmans will. I don't want that. You don't want that, especially given the apparent sabotage you just told me about. By the way, you're silly to think the same thing isn't happening here. No matter what state of disrepair this place is in, there's too damned much coincidence for every machine here to break down in some sort of perverse chain reaction. Think about that."

Obviously, she hadn't thought about it because her eyes went wide and lips parted. "My potatoes."

"Probably. You should look more closely into where those came from."

"Well, they came from—"

He put up a hand. "Let me finish, please."

She closed her mouth and nodded but still didn't seem convinced.

"I have some money of my own, but I also have a trust fund. I always assumed I'd never meet its terms. My parents adjusted it the year I stepped foot on that cruise ship. The terms were designed to force me back home, but I learned a trade and kept moving. Legally, I'm allowed to be here for another few months at most because technically, I'm still under contract with my last employer. They've just given me room to wander with the understanding that I can be recalled at any time. Good deal for them because they're not paying me at the moment, and good deal for me because I don't have to work in their home city. Trust me, South Africa is hot, but Miami has a special sort of stickiness you never really get used to."

Colleen sighed. "Alan, get on with it." She leaned back in her seat, draping her arms over the rests.

He'd need to replace that thing. That'd be his first order of business. Well, maybe second or third. First, he needed to run those wires and install the can lights in the front half of Colleen's little house. He had the cans out in his truck along with some drywall, just waiting to be rained on.

"Right, of course. The terms of the trust fund disbursement are that I establish a permanent residence—"

"That seems easy enough. You have a lease."

"Not quite. Second, I need to get married."

"Well, that's perfectly draconian."

"You have to understand my father. He thinks the family is the guts of the business, and if we kids aren't loyal—if we don't stick around and join the ranks—then how does that look to outsiders?"

"Oddly enough, I don't think outsiders care. I have a little brother, you know. He's a sheriff's deputy. He doesn't give a hot damn about this farm beyond the apples and pears that make the hard cider he loves so much."

No one around the farm talked about Jacob, and Alan couldn't tell if that was a good thing or a bad one.

"I guess I'm a third-generation farmer on both sides," she continued. "Daddy's grandfather was a career soldier, and he didn't settle down in the area until Daddy's father was nearly grown. Granddad's farm was very small. My legacy probably isn't as impressive as yours, but a lot of folks put their cash in Daddy's care to make this venture something to be proud of, and ... well, it's not. You can't imagine what that guilt is like for me. Maybe Daddy doesn't feel it, but I do every time I visit my granddad's grave. He worked himself to death for his family, and everything he had to show for that work he gave to Daddy. We're still babies at this. Tell me, how many generations of Prevosts have been cultivating rooibos and stomping on grapes to make that award-winning wine, huh?"

He rubbed his chin and drew his bottom lip between his teeth. "I see your point. But look, I see it as an investment. You get the farm on its feet, placate your restless ancestors ... "

She scowled at him. "Don't be a jerk. I'm as serious as an Easter mass. You don't know guilt the way I do."

She was right. He liked to prevent regrets as much as he could, so guilt wasn't a frequent station for him. "I apologize."

She nodded.

"And my father would rage spectacularly." They had never seen eye to eye on much of anything. Alan had stopped trying to please the man long ago and had only thought about acquiring the farm for the Prevost operation to show that even if he didn't want South Africa to be his home base anymore, he did still care about his family's success. But the problem was he had never given any thought to his own success. He'd been transient for so long he had forgotten what it meant to make goals and plans—to strive for something beyond making it home at five o'clock for a strong drink.

"And move on at the socially correct time? On what grounds are you going to annul the marriage? Fraud?"

He'd already given it some thought. Didn't make a difference to him one way or another. "I assumed you would file. Pick whatever reason you'd like, and I'll sign off."

"So, you get your trust fund. I get to fix my farm."

"That's the long and short of it." God, he hated lying to this woman. It left him feeling cold in a way he'd never experienced when he told his mother fibs about his plans, especially now that he knew why Colleen was fighting for the farm in the first place.

She shook her head and clucked her tongue. "Not quite. You forget, I own only about forty percent of the shares in this place. We're small and messy, but we're incorporated as a C-corp to keep the land assets separate from the business itself. I have some decision-making ability operations-wise, but the big stuff? I'm not technically allowed to do it without shareholder approval."

"Who all has shares?"

"Daddy, myself, Jacob has some, my mother has some, and there are a few investors from way back when who could probably be bought out."

"You've thought about this, then?"

She did that elegant shrug again. "One of the very first things I did after taking this position was sit down and chart out where all the money was going. Yeah, Daddy got an infusion of investor money shortly after the farms split, but I don't see why they should be skimming profits all these years later. They've been paid a hundred times over."

"That's an interest rate I don't like. So, you'll consider it?"

She scoffed and used the chair arms to push to standing. She grabbed her mug and walked to the credenza. "I think the proposition is insane, but … with some cash, I may be able to incentivize Daddy to take the retirement he so needs."

"Ouch." And he thought *he* was being mercenary.

"I know. It sounds brutal, but let's be real. The farm is an embarrassment. It's nothing like my mother's family's dairy farm. They were small, but the place had a heart. This place … " She groaned. "It's like Tin Man from *The Wizard of Oz*. Before he died, Daddy's father used to say that when the heart stopped beating, the farm would die. He'd say it every time he came over, and I didn't know why he kept harping on it. I thought maybe he was senile."

Alan tented his fingers. "You think your grandfather had a premonition?"

"No. I think he just knew Daddy really well, and so do I. Daddy won't see reason and trim the fat we desperately need to be rid of, so maybe I'll take the decision-making chores away from him."

It *did* sound brutal, but coming from Colleen, it was sexy as hell.

While her back was turned as she fixed her second cup of coffee, she didn't see the grin he couldn't suppress. She also couldn't see his quick readjustment of his crotch.

"And if I can pick up the shambles around here and get the heart beating again, I may even be able to pay you back before one or both of us have a foot in the grave." She turned, and her grin was hopeful.

He wore a smile, too, but it was forced. He'd forgotten about that "paying back" part.

"Mmm hmm."

"Can I think about it a couple of hours? I still need to take that check to the bank."

"Of course, Colleen." Anything to get some space from her, since apparently he was having a hard time mustering up his common sense when she stood near him. "I need to go clean up the mess I left at your house while the sun is out. Clouds are looking a little suspicious and I don't want to be in your attic in the dark."

She snapped her fingers. "Yeah. About that, what are you doing to my house? I thought I told you not to waste time with it when so much stuff needs to be done on the farm."

"Listen, we'll talk later, but think about it. Why fix the harvester when there's nothing to harvest at the moment?"

She rolled her eyes and groaned. "Touché, Mr. Prevost."

"Alan. We're friendlier than that."

"We *were*."

He ignored the slight. "I'll be done with the wiring in a few days, and then I'll start in this building. I'm certain the insurance company will appreciate the updates."

"How much is all this going to cost me?"

His immediate impulse was to say, "Don't worry about it," but that would only raise her hackles. Instead, he said, "It'll cost more if you *don't* do it."

She seemed to consider it as she sipped her coffee. "You're reasonable. I like reasonable people."

He wanted her to like a few other things about him, too, in the same way he really liked her. When he'd untangled his limbs from hers and eased off the bed, he'd thought he'd gotten his need for her out of his system. He'd thought maybe it was just a mental lapse brought on by hormones and that once he'd had her, he could focus on business.

Nope. That caveman impulse to get her as naked as possible was still there, along with a few other ones.

He swallowed. "So, I guess you're not firing me just yet?"

"That begs to be decided. How about we meet at the diner at one? You can buy me a late lunch, and in the meantime, I'll try to talk myself out of doing this."

Out of it?

Coffee mug and FedEx envelope in hand, she strode out of the office and down the hall in her squeaky boots, leaving him scratching his head.

Really? Just like that, she was going to marry him?

She really was practical. He wasn't deluded enough to think he was so great of a catch that getting her claws into him was a good deal for any other reason. He was a man without a home. A wanderer. Lacked her class and education. Sure, he had a little money, but what woman would want him for anything besides that?

He owned enough clothing to pack into two large duffel bags and paid other people to wash it. He couldn't remember his own grandmother's birth date. He knew nothing of politics, didn't follow the news, and never cut his hair until it caught in his seatbelt strap.

A catch, he was not, but he hoped she didn't notice just yet.

CHAPTER SEVEN

Kate raised her right hand and said in a sotto voice, "I do solemnly swear under penalty of being maimed and furthermore forfeiting my upcoming raise that I will never speak to any person beyond the ones in this vehicle about the nature of your marriage."

"So help me God," Alan said from the driver's seat with a chuckle.

"So help me God," Kate repeated.

"You want me to run inside the diner and get some rice to throw?" Pixie asked. She hadn't even taken off her work apron. Colleen had poked her head into the diner door and asked if she could borrow her for an hour, and the woman hadn't even asked "For what?" Something in Colleen's expression must have intrigued her, because she told her boss, "Be right back," and hopped in Alan's truck with no further ado. She and Kate stood as witnesses to the blessed union at City Hall, which put the magistrate into a bit of a tizzy.

Just as well. It'd put Colleen into a tizzy, too. What the hell was she doing? Did she really just marry a guy for his money like some kind of gold-digging tramp?

"I didn't know you were dating anyone, Colleen," the magistrate had said. "No offense, but I thought you would never get married. And I just saw your brother. He didn't breathe one word about it. Does he approve? You'd think Jacob would have said something."

She didn't know how to respond to that, but fortunately, Alan had. He really was charming, the jerk.

"Spur of the moment kind of thing," he'd said. "We were driving by on the way back from lunch and I said, 'Baby, let's do it.' I don't think she believed me until I paid the fee for the license."

She had just nodded. What the hell else could she do?

"You want some cake to take home, Colleen?" Pixie climbed down from the back seat of the crew cab, shut the door, and stepped in front of Colleen's open window. "Or are you still set with the chocolate?"

"What kind of cake and where's it from?" Kate asked sagely.

"Vanilla with coffee cream cheese frosting. It's from the bakery."

"Then *no*," she and Kate said in unison.

"What am I missing here?" Alan killed the engine on the truck, obviously believing the hens were going to cluck a while.

Pixie rolled her eyes. "Zoe Miller owns the bakery, right? Sweet little thing. I taught her, just like I did Colleen and Adam way back in the prehistoric era. They were all in the same class."

"Well thanks, lady. I'm thirty-two, not a dinosaur." No shame in putting her age right out there now, especially since Alan had seen it on her birth certificate. At least she wasn't thirty-five and a migrant like *him*.

"How old do you think that makes me? I've got bunions older than you. Anyhow, Alan, Colleen boycotts Whitman-affiliated products for the sake of her self-esteem."

She scoffed. "Right, that's why. Doesn't have *anything* to do with the fact that me bolstering their bottom line would be like a panhandler giving change to a millionaire."

Alan snorted, but he had the good grace to turn his face toward the driver's side window.

"Dick," she muttered.

"Right now? Bit early in the day to be starting a honeymoon, but if it'd please you … " He motioned to turn the key in the ignition.

"You wish."

Actually, *she* did. Unfortunately, they'd crossed the line from the no-strings-attached stage into something … well, legal. If they had sex again, it wouldn't even be a sin, and somehow, that felt wrong.

"Hate to break up the reception early," Kate said, leaning into the gap between the front seats. "I've got a three o'clock appointment to greet. Remember, Colleen? That guy from the state agriculture department who's putting that booklet together?"

"Dammit." Colleen pounded the dashboard. There was always something. God forbid she step off the property for five minutes. She couldn't keep running the farm with such a small operations staff or else she'd start thinking the idea of work-life balance was a fairy tale.

"Hey!" Alan rubbed the dashboard as if the thing had nerve endings and tender feelings. "Pick on someone who can fight back."

"Gladly, moneybags. I'll pick on *you*. That guy is visiting to find out what we're growing and selling this year for those folks who want to buy local and yada, yada."

"I see the problem."

"Yes, so I'll need more than fifteen minutes to get my lies straight. I'm not good at it."

He laughed and started the engine back up. "I love a woman who can't lie."

"And she sure can't." Pixie backed away and waved them off. "When you need a good laugh, ask her about that time in fifth grade when Adam Whitman and some other little knucklehead got her caught up in a glue and glitter scheme that had her scraping the undersides of desks for two weeks."

Alan turned to her.

Colleen said, "Nope," and fixed her eyes straight ahead.

Back at the farm, they all debarked the truck without saying a word.

Alan continued down the path to Colleen's house after pressing some bored-looking farm laborer into apprenticing him for the day.

Kate ran off to check phone messages.

Colleen took a bracing breath and turned her cell phone back on, fully expecting an inundation of messages from bill collectors.

Three voicemails, all from Greg.

"Oops. Forgot about him." She called him.

"Oh. My. God. If I didn't know any better, I'd say you were trying to avoid me, love. That's not nice."

"Hey, lay off. I had a rough morning."

If by "rough" she meant the feel of Alan's chin stubble against her cheek when he'd rolled over at around dawn, then she wasn't telling a lie. The rest of the morning had been merely *inconvenient*.

"Got the check this morning, by the way. I'll dig in after close of the business day. Thanks for dropping those samples off."

"Great. The folks in the design department will certainly appreciate your expeditiousness. Hey. You sound cheerful. What's up?"

"Can't a girl just be happy?" Things were looking up. She didn't have to find a crossroad to bury a hoodoo bag at and strike a bargain with the devil to make payroll for the month. And, well, there was that small matter of a man kissing her senseless in front of the magistrate like he actually *meant* that whole "your bride" *shtick*.

She could barely feel her feet afterward.

"You usually restrict your happiness to the inside. Anyhow, I know you're busy, but what are you doing right now?"

"I've got a meeting at three, but I'm free after that."

"Well, come hang out. Some of the gang is here and would love to see you. We're shooting until around six and hoping to get a little rain. If we don't get any, we'll have to set up the hoses and sprinklers."

They may have been the only people in Washington State hoping for rain. The Skagit Valley had been getting nothing *but* rain lately.

"Maybe I will if I find time to change my clothes. I wouldn't want to sully your reputation by popping over in my *grubbies*." The same grubbies she'd just gotten married in—storm cloud rubber boots included.

"I've never seen you anything but impeccable."

"Life on the farm, Greg. Life on the farm. See ya." She ended the call, sighing as she tucked the phone into her back pocket and startling a bit as Kate pushed the outer door open.

"You better get in here. We've got a problem," Kate said.

"Of course we do. That's what we grow here. Apples and pears and problems."

Kate sighed and lowered her voice to a whisper. "This problem has eighty-proof breath and a bone to pick. Claims you owe him a paycheck."

Colleen pressed the heels of her palms against her closed eyes. "Have I used up my f-word quota for today?"

"Yes."

"Then, *shit*."

"Do you owe him a check?"

"No. Not a penny. I laid him off, what, six weeks ago?"

"More than that, I think."

"Yeah. I paid him his due and more besides. Don't worry. I'll get rid of him before the agriculture guy gets here."

Kate held the door open for her, and she straightened her spine before walking into the carpeted reception area. She made eye contact with her former part-time custodian but willed her body to slow—to take her time.

He was on *her* time after all and not the other way around. She'd always had trouble with that concept.

She paused at the mat, pulling her feet through the boot scrapers and brushing her not-actually-dirty hands clean on her shirt.

Finally, she turned to Marlon Miller, and in her blandest, flattest voice, said, "We're not hiring right now, but if you check back in two or three weeks, there may be an opening for someone with a valid driver's license."

Which he didn't have. If he'd driven out there, Colleen would have no choice but to call the sheriff because everyone in Emerald Springs knew the guy probably hadn't had a valid license since around the time the Supersonics went defunct. Marlon, also known as the town drunk, was the ever-perky Zoe Miller's paternal unit. He'd been on the skids for years, but Split Acres had needed a handyman, and on paper the man was qualified. In real life, however, he preferred his screwdrivers to be fruity orange drinks and not tools.

"Don't need a job. Need my *money*."

"What happened?" Colleen flipped through the stack of mail on Kate's desk idly, not really reading anything but using the action as a control device. She'd learned that trick from Greg. If she didn't appear to be giving her complete attention to the situation, the annoying person would get fed up at not having a podium and microphone to exploit and would eventually go away. "Did you lose your wallet again?"

"Got my wallet, but there's nothing in it. You gotta pay me."

She set the mail pile on the corner of Kate's desk and crossed her arms over her chest, now making eye contact with the lush. "Maybe you need some help with your memory. Have a seat and I'll get you a copy of your last pay stub and the cancelled check that's attached to it."

He waved a hand at her, dismissively. "Ah, I don't need that mess. Just give me a little something to tide me over until my unemployment kicks in."

"Maybe you haven't noticed lately, but this is a business, not a charity. Since I'm in a good mood today, I'll give you something better than a five-dollar bill."

"Ten?"

She winked. "Better." Colleen picked up Kate's desk phone and dialed the number she'd had to commit to memory.

"Adam Whitman, Emerald Tea Farm."

She launched into it without further pleasantries. "Adam, it's Colleen. I know you're busy, but your future father-in-law is three sheets to the wind and in my reception area. I believe he drove here. Either you or the sheriff needs to come get him. I figured you'd want first dibs."

Adam swore an oath and sighed. "Thanks for the call. Can you hold him for fifteen minutes?"

Glancing at the analog clock on the wall behind Kate's desk, Colleen said, "No," without hesitation. "I've got a three o'clock appointment, and I hate to say it, but he's bad for business."

"Business." Marlon sputtered his lips behind her. "Always wondered what one of those looked like."

"Better hurry," she said to Adam, rubbing her eyes again. "He's starting to talk gibberish. I wouldn't want to have to turn the hose on him."

"Coming!" Adam hung up.

She perched her rear on the edge of Kate's desk and watched the man pace.

Back when he'd first started, he'd always been on time. Efficient. Could fix pretty much anything and wasn't averse to getting his hands dirty when they needed some extra bodies out in the fields or orchards. But then something happened, and what, Colleen didn't know. His downward slide started with him arriving at work with red eyes and a few minutes late. Next, he was found napping on the job. The foreman would go hours, waiting on some small repair, and Marlon would never show up. Didn't respond to walkie-talkie hails. Then there were the days he'd be flat-out drunk at work, yelling at the staff, and sometimes passing out and sleeping off the booze in the barn.

Having to cut his hours then lay him off had been a relief, and not just for financial reasons. She kept giving this man chances because he was of a certain age—just like Daddy and Richard and Sam Whitman. He had the foundation to be respectable or at least decent. And she thought some tough love and maybe a little kindness would get him on his way. But if his own daughter couldn't straighten him out, then it wasn't Colleen's job, either.

A vehicle door slammed, and before the owner of the vehicle could stride in, she directed her gaze to the agitated man and said, pointedly, "If I find you here in my office again, harassing my staff, I'll call the sheriff's office."

When he showed her his favorite finger, she barely resisted the temptation to show two of her own.

Adam stepped in, scanned the room briefly, and rolled his eyes at his beloved's father, who now stood in the corner filling a paper cone with water from the cooler, as calm as he pleased.

"Zoe and I owe you one, Colleen. Need anything, anything at all," he grabbed the man by the crook of his arm and pulled him toward the door, "just let us know."

She waved him away. "I don't do *quid pro quo*, Adam. I learned that lesson in fifth grade, remember?"

Raking his free hand through his hair, he nodded. "Yeah." He pulled some more then paused at the doorway. "I can't remember the last time I saw you wearing jewelry. You get a new ring?"

"She got a new husband," Kate said with a snicker. "Big, fine one. He's around here somewhere."

Colleen's heart suddenly beat in overdrive.

Color flooded Adam's face, and he loosened his grip on Marlon just long enough for the man to make a run for it through the open door. "Damn it. Hey, Colleen? Why don't you call Zoe and set something up for dinner, huh? We can catch up. I feel like I should have heard about there being a guy. Jacob should have said something, I would think."

She didn't respond, which was just as well because Adam shouted, "Wait! Do *not* get in that truck," and rushed from the office.

"Think we should help him?" Kate asked, wringing her hands.

Colleen swallowed, regaining her bearings, and shrugged. She strode down the corridor and stepped over the sleeping sheltie before she called back, "No. He needs the practice." *Oh my god. I really did marry a guy.*

"Colleen?" Kate called down the hall.

"Yeah?" Colleen waited in the doorway and watched Kate shuffle toward her. The fact she'd left her chair filled Colleen with a sense of foreboding.

Kate called back on the phone or paged her on the walkie-talkie. She didn't do heart-to-hearts.

Oh boy.

Colleen escaped into her office, out of the range of vision of the intern across the hall.

Kate followed her in and shut the door.

Colleen fixed her messy hair at the mirror beside the file cabinets and tried to ignore her secretary's knowing glare.

Kate wasn't one to be ignored. She cleared her throat.

"What?"

"How are you feeling?"

"About what?" Colleen asked blithely. She pulled open a file cabinet drawer and riffled through a stack of seed catalogues.

"You just married your farm custodian."

"Yup." Finding the catalog she needed, she carried it to her desk and sat.

Kate eased onto one of the spindly chairs in front of her. "Colleen of two years ago wouldn't have done it."

"Colleen of two years ago wasn't desperate."

"For what? Money or the man?"

Her jaw dropped, and Kate stood, leaned across the desktop, and nudged it back up. She patted Colleen's head and sat again.

"I've known you for a very long time, Colleen. I probably know you better than your own mother because you try to hide all the messy stuff from her."

"You're fired."

Kate brushed some lint off her farm polo shirt. "Why are you embarrassed all of a sudden?"

"I'm not." Colleen stared at the open catalog without actually seeing anything. The words and pictures all blurred.

"I get it. He's handsome. He's charming. He's not afraid of you. If he'd been anyone else, you wouldn't have done it."

"You don't know that. Maybe I am as desperate as you say, and I would have latched onto any warm body that got close." She'd tried for self-deprecating, but that was lost when it all came out in a whisper. She looked up, and Kate's gaze was soft.

Kate didn't have to speak.

"Did I do a bad thing?"

"Bad? No. I think you did a very messy thing, the two of you. Lord knows how it'll play out." Kate stood and shuffled toward the door. "Messy, but you're used to cleaning up messes, right?"

"Yeah."

The last thing she'd needed was another one, so why had she brought one down onto herself with barely a thought? That wasn't like her. She was a *thinker*. A planner.

This time, it was as if her brain hadn't even come into play with this decision.

CHAPTER EIGHT

"Colleen Sanders, you are a sight for sore eyes." Greg pulled her into his sandalwood-scented embrace and gave her a hug that could have reknit bones, should they have needed it.

"It's nice to be seen." She pulled back and smoothed her breezy silk top over her waist, trying for a grin and fearing the best she could manage was a half-hearted sneer. She hated being watched, and watched she was.

About half of the people in the loose congregation amassed at Emerald Paradise were resort staff and Emerald Springs residents. They knew Colleen, but had never seen her like *this*. Had never seen her in anything beyond her basic black and rain boots since she'd come home. For the other half, this was the Colleen they expected. All done up with a full slap of make-up, hair meticulously put up, and shoes that looked a bit inconvenient.

She wasn't even sure if she could manage a heel for five minutes, much less an hour these days, so she'd hedged and slipped into a pair of cute flats before slumping to her truck.

Alan had called down from the attic, "Are you off to the gallows, Colleen?"

She'd replied, "Yes," and he'd laughed up there in the rafters.

Some husband. *Faux* husband, anyway.

Thinking of her so-called husband/cash cow, she stuffed her ring hand into her slacks pocket. "So, what's going on?"

Greg pulled a khaki-colored cap over his salt-and-pepper hair and pushed his dark, horn-rimmed glasses up his narrow nose. "You saw the swatches, right?"

"I did. Interesting palette."

"There's some crazy stuff coming off the runways, so the design team slapped all those colors into the mix and hoped the artists could make 'em stick."

"Mmm hmm." Colleen eyed the models in their bright orange, red, and royal blue outerwear gear and suppressed a groan. In a whisper, she said, "You should have balanced out those colors with neutrals. Single block colors like that don't look good on people older than, oh, age twenty."

"Which is why we have eighteen-year-old models."

"Whose idea was this?"

He put his hands up, palms out, and widened his eyes. "You know it wasn't me. I spoke my opinion on the stuff, and the hip new creative director vetoed me. She's twenty-seven years old and made me feel about as unhip as Methuselah. I don't remember you ever being such a brat."

She bobbed her shoulders and crossed her arms. "I worked in operations. We worker bees tend to avoid histrionics. Remember? They cut into productivity."

"I love you, girl. Miss you so much." He wrapped his arm around her back and chafed her right arm.

"You taught me well, Mr. V.P."

"Yeah, fat lot of good that title does me if little twerps on a power trip who happen to be shaken out of the CEO's family tree get final say on the outerwear."

"I'm sure my patterns will go over swimmingly, then."

"Nah, prissy little creative director can't touch those. Everyone knows Greg is the boot master. There hasn't been a single season where one of your patterns hasn't sold out in every size. They wouldn't dare mess with the tried and true, especially given they're gonna lose boatloads of money on this outerwear campaign."

Greg's secretary paused in front of them, handed each a bottle of water and a fancy parchment-wrapped sandwich, then moved on in her pink pansy rain boots and matching hat.

"Hey, the pansies. I can't believe folks still have those," Colleen said, handing her unwanted gourmet Emerald Paradise sandwich to Greg, who unwrapped it and his own greedily.

"Friggin' starving. Been in my room putting out fires via Skype all day, but yeah, the pansies. We brought those back in the spring."

"Way to recycle, Greg."

"I hear recycling's hip." He tipped his water bottle toward her and grunted.

She uncapped it.

"Thanks, love. When do you think you'll get those sketches to the design crew?"

She drew her bottom lip between her teeth and worried it. Used to be she could crank out a design over her lunch break, but the cache of creativity wasn't endless. She'd worked in operations, not design, but occasionally she'd dream of kitschy, cutesy, cartoony things in her sleep and would wake up with a picture to draw. Greg had noticed the doodles on her desk one day and had kissed her on the cheek, telling her she'd saved his bacon. Then he'd run off with the sketches. A month later, those drawings showed up in the spring catalog's boot palette, and she'd ended up doing a few new designs each season after that until she quit. It was a fun diversion, and yeah, the extra money was nice.

Lately, though, she hadn't been getting much REM sleep in which inspirational dreams were possible. In fact, the last time she dreamed—that she could remember—had been last night. She'd dreamed of a blue-eyed man twirling a wrench and smiling at her like she was an unexpected Christmas present.

Even thinking of that man and that little lecture from Kate made her cheeks burn.

"Three designs, probably Friday," she said when the pulse in her ears stopped pounding so loudly.

"Do I get a sneak peek?"

"Are you offering me the chance to bypass your veto? I don't think you've ever done that before."

Greg shrugged. "You've never given me a reason to say no. We need more doodlers down in the art department. They don't do whimsy the way you do."

"Lower your voice when you talk about whimsy, will you? I've got a reputation to uphold around here."

He grinned. "Sorry. Forgot. Cold Colleen. Scary. Boo."

She laughed in spite of herself. "Funny. I gotta get out of here before I'm spotted by a Whitman. They might charge me a toll or something."

Greg shifted his sandwiches to his left hand and wrapped his right one around her for another squeeze. "We're here until Thursday. Give me a call if you have time to buy an old friend lunch."

"Or vice versa."

He winked and saluted her with a sandwich. "You name the place, and I'll be there with the Markson Outfitters credit card. The folks in accounting won't quibble. All I have to say is 'Colleen' and they go 'oh' and continue surfing Tumblr on their phones."

"Really oughtta tighten up that wifi firewall."

He shrugged and sauntered to the trash can situated near the end of the craft services table. "Maybe you can come take your job back and handle it for me. I'm a busy guy."

Colleen shook her head and strode toward the path leading through the woods to the parking lot. "Bye, Greg. I've got a farm to run."

"The offer still stands, love," he called after her. "Anytime you want. Just give me twenty-four hours notice so the housekeeping crew can peel the plastic off your office furniture."

She waved behind her and increased her pace. If she stayed much longer, she just might get talked into something she knew damn well wasn't in her heart to do anymore. She was a farmer, not a paper-pusher.

• • •

Alan wished Colleen hadn't been in such a hurry to change her clothes after her mysterious meeting. She'd rushed through the door at six, already pulling the gauzy shirt overhead as if it were causing her great distress, and he'd stood there, holding loose wires and gaping until she disappeared down the hallway in her camisole and unbuttoned slacks. He'd had one mind to follow her for teasing him like that, but upon hearing her relieved sounding groan from the master bedroom, opted to give her some space.

He slid the sheath of trust fund release paperwork across her coffee table and dug his chopsticks back into the pint of vegetable lo mein they shared.

They'd had sex, after all. They could certainly swap a little spit.

"Kate said that's everything the lawyer faxed." She set down her bowl of wonton soup and riffled through the paper stack. "As if it isn't enough. Some of this stuff isn't handily available, and the rest seems ... " She squinted at one particular page. "Excessive."

"I'm not arguing with that, but ... "

The gold of her ring glinted in the living room's much improved light, and he couldn't help but to fixate on the cheap thing. They'd grabbed them from a small department store near the diner on the way back to Emerald Springs, and they'd basically picked the first two that didn't need resizing. Suddenly, he felt ashamed of himself. Up until now in his life, he'd given women's jewelry approximately zero thought, but ignorant as he was on the subject, he knew that ring was wrong ... even for a fake wife.

"What?" she asked, setting down the papers.

"What kind of ring do you want? I'm philosophically opposed to diamonds, so what's your birthstone?"

"Ring?" As if the idea were a foreign concept to her, she crinkled her nose.

"Yes, ring. You need a ring befitting a ... " He was going to say "multi-millionaire's wife," but that seemed crass. He swallowed and tried again. "Something a little better than you could get in a Las Vegas five-and-dime."

Her grin reached her eyes, deepening the charming creases beside them and broadcasting her genuine state of amusement. "You've spent much time coordinating Vegas weddings?"

"Coordinating, no, but I've witnessed enough of them. Whenever I was on cruise ships with a Los Angeles port of call longer than a day, I'd end up with a bunch of jokers who'd want to weekend in Vegas. I've been best man more times than I care to remember."

Her smile drew in a bit. "How many of those marriages lasted beyond the weekend?"

He shrugged. "Most did, but longer than that I can't say. Living on a cruise ship isn't exactly like real life."

"You've visited ports all over the world. I've been as far east as Maine but haven't been farther north or west than Alaska."

"And south?"

"L.A., of course."

"You want to travel?"

He would have pegged Colleen as being too impatient for it. All the waiting around for planes, for luggage. Standing in lines to see sights, not knowing the local language. But all that stuff made it fun sometimes, too.

"I wish I were more worldly. I would like to travel, I guess … with the right guide. "

Me. Seemed obvious to him, though she may not have agreed. He was pretty sure his sister Kimi used to sing a song about that from some Disney movie. There was a magic carpet involved.

His head swam at the thought of his little sister. She'd be so crushed that he'd gotten married and she wasn't there, but this wasn't a *real* marriage. Maybe he'd never even tell her.

"I think I'd feel stressed-out for leaving so much responsibility behind. There's always so much to do, and if I'm not here—"

"It won't get done. Right. That guilt again, huh?" He may not have courted guilt, but he knew it. He'd felt the nagging and unreasonable discomfort of wrongdoing after he'd left home all those years ago. He'd never forget the look on his mother's face when he'd slung that duffel bag over his shoulder and climbed in his friend's Jeep for the airport. She'd looked at him like he was some sort of traitor and not a son who needed to find his own way.

He'd thought of all people, she'd understand the desire to roam, but instead, she'd turned out to be the person most opposed to his departure.

Maybe it was because she feared that like her, he wouldn't return home. Maybe she'd broken her own mother's heart by leaving France with only her packed knapsack and a passport.

Maybe his children, should he have any, would do the same someday.

Children? He'd reached thirty-five without giving a single thought to offspring, but they sort of came with the package deal, right? Settle down, own some land, build a house, fill it with kids.

Colleen's hand reaching for the egg roll bag in front of him stirred him from his reverie. He swirled his noodles with his chopsticks and bobbed his head toward the stack of legal forms. "I didn't realize you'd have to change your name. I'm sorry."

"Well, they make it tricky for you to play pretend, anyway. I guess I'll cope. It'll be a few weeks before all the official documentation starts working its way around, but for all intents and purposes, the moment the Social Security office gets its copy of the marriage certificate, I'm Colleen Prevost. Then I get a new driver's license. Wanted a new picture anyway." She rolled her eyes. "I'll go stand in line at the Social Security office tomorrow. Should be a blast."

Colleen Prevost. Those names sounded good together, and as far as wives went, he'd certainly outdone his brother, whose trophy wife spoke three languages: whine, cry, and beg. Sure, she was pretty, but pretty only went so far with Alan. Hell, if he'd actually been looking for a marriageable woman, Colleen would have hit all the right buttons for him. Gorgeous. Smart. Practical. She'd make a hell of a partner for someone if they'd let her be that.

"I know you'd rather be doing other things," he said, accepting the eggroll half she offered.

"Hoped to see Greg again before he and the crew headed back to Seattle."

"Greg?"

"My boss of six years before I returned to the funny farm. He and some of my old coworkers are at the resort shooting last-minute images for the fall catalog."

Her expression had softened and her eyes took on a faraway look at the mention of this Greg—this *crew*—he hadn't known existed in her past. He plucked a snow pea from the noodles and chewed it contemplatively. "I didn't realize you'd worked elsewhere."

"If I hadn't, this place wouldn't be afloat right now. Sometimes Greg sends me some freelance, and pays me well over the market rate for it. I think he pities me. Actually," she brought her wrist in front of her face and squinted at her stainless steel watch's face, "I probably need to get started on that assignment soon."

Pity wasn't the first word that came to mind. Any man doing Colleen favors had to be doing it because he wanted to.

"Hopefully you won't have to do too much more of that. Once the paperwork is in, the cash will be disbursed fairly quickly. Just a matter of going through all the channels. Bet that conversion rate'll be hell."

"So, what else do I need to take care of tomorrow?"

Right. That. "Uh … " He moved some of the papers aside and found the one of interest. "Aside from the name change items, I have to establish residency by being listed as co-owner on any real estate you own."

"That'll be easy. I own this little house outright in the same way my brother owns that cottage out near the orchards. The farm property, though, that's the tricky bit. When I took the job, Daddy and Mom retained half, and I have the other."

"So … "

She chewed her bottom lip a moment. "I'll call my lawyer in the morning. Washington is a community property state, but I acquired the land before the marriage. Then there's the issue of my farm shares. I think I have to transfer some to you so you'll have voting rights. Before now, we've never had anyone marry into the family, so this has never come up. Daddy would probably have an answer, but he'll find out about our state of matrimony soon enough once I start running errands tomorrow."

He set down his chopsticks once again and now pulled his bottle of Tsingtao beer closer. "Then perhaps we should get our story straight. About when we met and how long we courted. That sort of thing."

She blew out a ragged breath and pried the edges of her fortune cookie wrapper open. "I hate this. Okay. How long were you in the area before you came here to work?"

"A few months locally, and a bit more total in the Pacific Northwest."

"No one's going to believe this because I haven't even been on a date in two years, but we'll say we met two months ago at the diner, and you bought me cake."

"You fell in love over cake?"

"That part would be believable. The unbelievable part would be the fact I let you pay for it."

"Ah." He could see that.

"I'm known for my practicality, so we can just say we didn't see the sense in waiting if we knew we were going to be each other's happily-ever-after." She didn't bother squelching the snort that came after that, and oddly, he felt a bit bruised by it.

"You don't think I could be someone's happily-ever-after, Colleen?"

She had the decency to look contrite, but her smile lingered. "I don't doubt you can. The old saying is 'there's someone for everyone.' Hell, Daddy proved that to be true, and I'm here as the magnificent product of that coupling. I just think if I had a forever guy, I wouldn't find him this way. This isn't … *normal*."

Oh, it'd be even less normal soon enough. By the time Joe caught wind of the upheaval they had in store, she'd *beg* him to buy her out completely. He could handle Joe, but now he wasn't so sure about Colleen. He may get the farm, but he'd also get a bonus gift of a broken heart, given the game they were playing.

Well. He'd always been able to fix anything. He'd just have to find a patch for that, too.

"I see." He sipped his beer and watched her cheeks flush as he swallowed. Shame, perhaps? Of what?

"So, regarding the matter of our separate addresses … "

"We don't actually *have* to live together if that's what you're implying. We just need the same address on paper."

"It would make sense if you lived with me while your house is being repaired."

She shook her head. "Last time I lived with a guy, my favorite underwear kept turning up missing."

"I don't want to wear your underwear, Colleen." Get in them, though? Definitely and often. He thought he'd made that clear in front of the magistrate with that bit of public groping.

"Let's broach this topic again later. I think shacking up would be overkill, but we can brainstorm something. I guess we'll have to once the wedding announcement hits the paper. People will expect to see your truck parked here overnight." She cringed.

Why was that idea so distasteful to her?

"Okay." He took a long sip of beer and watched her pick at her cuticles. "Last, there's the small matter of me going to Emerald Tea for a job before I landed here. People will be suspicious. Will doubt my intentions."

She hadn't considered that. He could tell by her gaping jaw. "I didn't realize you'd gone there first."

Let's try not to dig too deep a hole here. "They grow tea. I know tea."

"And you thought, what? That you'd work your way up from farm laborer to V.P.?"

"That was more or less the plan, yes."

"I see. So, we're just your sloppy seconds, huh?" She balled her cookie's little fortune slip into a tiny speck and flicked it onto the coffee table. "Split Acres comes in second place, yet again. I should be used to that feeling, but there's always a little bit of burn to losing everything to them."

"Colleen, you have to understand I didn't know anything about Split Acres until I queried over there. Don't take it personally."

"Hard not to."

"I get that. I do. But what are we going to say?"

She pulled her legs under her rear to stand. "Anything before the marriage, I plan on playing dumb about. The rest is up to you. Just let me know what lies I need to keep up with."

He followed her into the dark kitchen and watched her aggressively shove the remnants of their dinner into the refrigerator. What had gotten into her all of a sudden?

She let the door close with a soft snap and turned to face him, wiping her hands on the front of the grubby shirt she'd changed into. "I need to get some work done before bed."

Oh. Of course she did. She had said she had some freelance assignment to take care of, so why was he feeling so abruptly dismissed?

Ah, yes. He'd just been whammed by the ice queen. Cold Colleen.

His wife.

There she was. The woman everyone else feared, and now for some reason he did, too.

The lump in his throat seemed to cut off his words. He swallowed twice then managed, "Right. I'll be over around sunup to work on wiring."

She stepped past him toward the little office installed where the sunroom had once been. "Don't rush over. Long day ahead and I don't want plaster falling on my face while I sleep."

"Eight, then."

"Suit yourself."

She turned her back and walked away.

CHAPTER NINE

Colleen pressed the phone against her ear and said, "When is Daddy next due back on the farm?"

"Hold on, Mrs. Prevost. Let me pull the calendar." Kate giggled on her end.

Colleen rolled her eyes and set her forehead against the desktop, pounding it a few times for good measure. Who knew it would be so easy to wipe away an identity she'd spent thirty-two years building? On Monday, she'd met a man. Now on Wednesday, she had his last name. With a marriage certificate and driver's license, she was well on the way to getting a new Social Security card. In the meantime, she had a receipt that would do for all intents and purposes, and a spanking new driver's license with a picture just as bad as the previous one.

Her lawyer had said, after about two minutes of non-stop laughing, that Alan's residency requirement could be satisfied simply enough. He just needed to be added to the deed and tax records. If it weren't for that whole "lawyer-client confidentiality" thing, the guy probably would have been spreading her business all over town. Colleen Sanders married a guy with a trust fund, and a *farmer* no less? Who would have thunk it?

With just a bit of notarizing and faxing, the farm would be well on its way to solvency, thanks to Alan.

She was already plotting ways to pay him back with interest. If they could get those greenhouses up and running and renovate that vacant outbuilding, they just might be able to fill some voids in the market in time for it to matter.

All they had left for the year, really, was fruit. So maybe it was time to stick their toes in some warmer waters—produce some commodities that wouldn't be so dependent on the whims of Mother Nature ... or saboteurs.

What Alan had said about saboteurs targeting Split Acres hadn't set well with her. She'd been mulling over the idea nonstop since turning in the night before. Who would do such a thing? Who would want to trip them up when they were already on their asses? And to what end?

Obviously, she hadn't slept well.

Kate came back on the line. "He'll actually be in on Friday. There's a zoning board meeting or something he needs to do some schmoozing at."

"Damn it. I need to be at that. We may need to get some new permissions so we can manufacture here."

"You gonna let me in on the loop, or should I wait to read about it in the company newsletter along with your marriage announcement?"

"Funny." That guy she married was somehow already in her house when she'd rolled out of bed from her fitful sleep, installing the new grounded outlets into the kitchen walls. He'd already had the coffee perking with help of a long extension cord to the hallway. She hadn't acknowledged him beyond reaching around his waist to get a spoon from the utensil drawer for her sugar. And he hadn't moved. Just got in her way, making her get right up on him to serve herself in her own damn kitchen.

Although, in hindsight, his proximity wasn't that bad a thing to wake up to. He'd looked wonderful and alert, even with sleep-tousled hair, those loose-fitting jeans, and a bleach-splattered t-shirt that read *Duchess Cruise Lines, Panama*. The man could probably wear a garbage bag and look just as good, not that Colleen was paying much attention. He was like Greg: a peer. Someone she did business with and occasionally received money from. Difference there was she hadn't had mind-blowing *sex* with Greg. Any kind of sex, actually, or even the desire to. Alan just hit all her switches that way, and denying her attraction to him would be a classic case of the lady protesting too much.

She'd had one mind to grab his ass there at the coffee maker, but then she remembered why she was mad at him.

"We'll walk and talk, okay? Need to print a couple of checks, and we can take the *Mule* out to the greenhouses."

"You mean the greenhouse *foundations*."

"Don't rain on my parade, Kate. I didn't sleep well."

"Then I'll go clean out your travel mug and fill it up. See you in a few."

There was a reason she had bent over backward to keep Kate a full-time employee, and that sort of empathy was exactly it.

Minutes later, Colleen made her way down the hall, stepped over Arfer, and joined Kate in the reception area. She grabbed her coffee off the desk corner and said, "I think it's time we innovate now that we have some funds to make it happen." She was at the door, hand already extended to push it open, when Kate said, "Uh … you might want to—"

And there stood Alan on the walkway, arms crossed, grinning at her.

"Your walkie-talkie was hot," Kate said with a snort.

Colleen slumped. Well, nothing for it. He knew his role. He was there to give the operation an injection of much needed cash, but she didn't really need his supervision while she spent it. She'd just pretend she was a brat at the shopping mall with her daddy's credit card.

"Do you need something?" she asked.

He shook his head, the grin not shrinking one iota. "No. I was nearby. Figured I'd ride along. See if I can offer any suggestions."

She narrowed her eyes and gave her head an emphatic shake. "For what?"

"Your innovations. I may have lived at sea for a lot of years, but you won't find many people who know more about modern farming than I do."

"And an electrician, too. Next thing you're going to tell me you're an accomplished painter and are an expert at *krav maga*."

His eyes rolled skyward. "Actually, I—"

"Nope." She walked past him toward the paved employee lot where she kept a Kawasaki Mule mini-truck parked for farm business.

She took the driver's seat and Alan graciously let Kate slip into shotgun position. When they were on the way down the dirt path, Colleen looked over her shoulder briefly and said, "We started construction on the greenhouses about ten years ago, but the market for hydroponic produce softened, so Daddy scrapped the plan. At the time, I didn't understand why he didn't just finish them and keep them sort of in his back pocket so he'd have them when the market bounced back for tomatoes and green lettuce, but Daddy's never been good at thinking ahead. He's all about the here and now."

"Tell me about it," Kate mumbled.

Alan leaned toward the front seat and said, "That must make him a peculiar sort of politician."

Colleen shook her head. "No. That makes him a perfectly typical politician, but maybe the gig will teach him the error of his ways. Anyhow, I think this is a great time to finish construction on the trio. Since we don't have many crops this year, we concentrate on getting them set up for the winter… and beyond."

"What'd you have in mind? Organic vegetables?"

"Not just that." She parked the Mule near the westernmost slab and turned the engine off.

Kate and Alan followed as she started the long walk around the perimeter.

"You see, after everything, I still believe in diversification. A variety of crops and rotating them as often as makes sense. But we can't afford to operate like the Whitmans do anymore. We need to be leaner. More nimble." She stopped at the rear of the slab and stepped up onto it.

"I think I know what you're getting at," Alan said, propping one foot atop the platform and crossing his arms over his chest again. "You want to move all the farming you can indoors. Less sprawl means fewer employees."

"Exactly. Thing is, they'd need to be more knowledgeable employees. No one here knows much about greenhouse farming, so we'd be learning together."

"And as the operation starts to grow again, the folks here now will be around to train the new hires whenever we make them."

She didn't like the sound of that "we," but she pressed on, now walking the second slab. "Right. But I don't want to do lettuce, and there are enough hothouse tomatoes in the valley to be seen from outer space. We need to farm some things that aren't conducive to outdoor growing in this area. Things that are hard to get up here during the winter."

"Like what, watermelons?" Kate looked up from the pad onto which she was scratching notes.

Good woman.

"Maybe. I haven't finished the market analyses yet, but there are some smaller varieties we may be able to manage indoors. I was also thinking of re-entering the floral trade. Mom did it on a small scale years ago but couldn't keep it up on her own, even though she was so good at it. Another layer of my guilt there. Ugh." Her stomach lurched.

"What happened?" Alan asked, and his brow furrowed with what looked like genuine curiosity.

The romantic part of her wanted to reward him for that, but her spiteful part smacked it silly and told it to shut up.

"It was just like when Richard proposed adding tea to the WhitSand Farm crops. The projections looked excellent, but it was too *other* for Daddy. A few years after the split, Mom suggested they expand the floral yields because they were so robust and would bring in good money, but Daddy didn't want the farm to be known for '*frou-frou* shit.'" She made air quotes with her fingers.

"I told your mother back then, and I'm telling you now," Kate said, "it's a damned good idea."

"Thank you. It'd take us a few years to go from seed to bloom, but the number of flower growers in this part of the state is quite small. If we convert that field," she pointed to the fallow field from *last* year's potato disaster and indicated the expanse, "and make it suitable for the tulips that grow so well here, we could use one of the greenhouses exclusively for other sorts of houseplants and flowers. Irises. Peace lilies. Poinsettias. Orchids, maybe. I love orchids."

She loved them so much, they'd been included in her boot designs twice—including the boots she was wearing at the moment.

"Okay, I'm with ya." Kate scribbled furiously on her pad again. "So we need to get the contractor out here for an updated quote ASAP. Now, what about that outbuilding you mentioned?"

"Right. I'm in contact with a woman out East who manufactures an organic cosmetics line. I met her at a conference last fall. We happened to be wearing the same boots and started chatting." She felt Alan's hand on the small of her back as she resumed her trek to the Mule. She couldn't tell if he was bored and eager for her to move along, or if he'd put his hand there in some sort of subconscious tic—that cuddle reflex again.

Either way, by the time they'd returned to the vehicle, he'd pulled his hand back.

"She manufactures everything from lipstick to soap, and talking to her, I wondered if we could find a new cross-section of customers if we sold direct to manufacturers. Things like dried fruit, honey—"

Alan placed a hand on her shoulder that was so gentle, her spine tingled. What was she going to say? God, she needed him to stop touching her.

"You have bees here?" he asked. "I haven't seen them."

Oh. She nodded. "Just a couple of hives in the orchards. Since we're basically killing off our crop production in the fields and therefore ceasing our pesticide use after this year, I thought maybe we could seed some clover out there and start some new hives. Anyhow, dried fruit, honey, floral extracts—the sort of stuff that's more valuable when refined."

"So you want to convert that empty outbuilding into a processing station."

"Exactly. Something separate from the crops we'll be phasing out. It's time we stopped selling straight to consumers and supermarkets when there's more stability in value-added goods."

"Hmm," Alan murmured from the backseat.

"What do you think?"

"I think you've given this a lot of thought."

"Worth your money?" She cranked the key and aimed the Mule toward the gravel path.

"Just may be. Can I sit down and look over your plans?"

"Don't trust me?" She clamped her teeth and tried not to steer the cart over potholes. If he were smart, he'd learn to just take her word for things. It'd save them all time and conversation. Greg had learned that lesson, though perhaps too late to admit it.

"Split Acres is a big farm. I just want to be sure we're using the assets we have in the most efficient manner. That we're not … overtaxing the *heart*, as you'd say."

"Right." *We* he'd said. Why did he keep saying *we*?

The prickling on the right side of her face made her glance over to see Kate giving her a tart look.

"What?"

"Nothing," Kate said.

"That's a pretty sour puss for *nothing*."

"Not my place, so I'm minding my tongue."

Colleen opened her mouth, closed it then locked her sights on the path. Whatever it was Kate had to say, she wasn't sure she wanted to hear it … and if she had to, maybe it'd be best in the privacy of her office. Again.

She dropped Alan off at his truck and resumed the drive back to the operations building, Kate glowering at her all the while. "What?"

Kate grunted. "You could be nice."

"Why?" She squinted at the building ahead and tried to place the familiar-looking vehicle parked to the left of her truck. The SUV's rear vanity plate read A CUPPA and she groaned, rolling her eyes.

"Sam Whitman," Kate sighed.

"He's tenacious, I'll give him that. What do you think he wants?"

"Probably here to check our pulse and see if the farm's death certificate needs a witness."

She parked the Mule in its spot, and before the two reached the office door, Sam intercepted them. He hiked his pants up to his distended belly and spread on that same sweet-as-cola smile he always wore. "Your girl in there didn't know how long you'd be gone. I had a little time, so I decided to hang out."

Colleen cut her eyes toward Kate, and Kate shrugged as she pulled the door open.

"What can I do for you, Sam?" Colleen asked, stopping inside the door. If he were waiting for an invitation back to her office, he wasn't going to get one. She didn't feel any particular unkindness toward the man, but she had a lot of work to do. He had to know that.

He raked a hand over Arfer's head as the lazy pooch approached the door. "I've got a business proposition for you."

"I'm not sure what we can do for you, but I'm genuinely curious. Lay it on me."

"Great. Really, you'd be doing me a big favor. I write a column about farming for the paper, you know. You probably read it."

Nope. In her defense, she'd tried once or twice but had found his pedantic prose to be as dry as Arizona in July. "I'm aware of it. Yeah." She let Arfer out to do his business and leaned against the door frame.

"Well, I thought it'd be good if I diversified the column a bit. Brought in some new voices."

"Meaning?"

"Can you turn a phrase, Colleen? It'd only need to be two hundred, two hundred fifty words."

Although she found it curious he'd pitch the idea to her at all, having a few inches of space in the local paper would be good press for the farm. Might even make her seem more approachable. "What would I have to do?"

He blew out a breath, as if relieved she didn't refuse outright. "Super easy. I give you a farm-related topic, and you opine on it."

"What's the catch?"

His gray eyebrows crept up, and his eyes went round. "Catch?"

Colleen nodded, slowly and unambiguously. "Are you going to tell me how much that amount of newspaper space is worth, and tell me who to write the check to?"

He shook his head and put his hands up. "No, no. Not at all. If it'll make you feel more comfortable, I'll tell you the truth. I'm asking lots of folks to contribute because I can't keep up with the weekly responsibility." He rubbed a hand over his shiny pate and sighed. "I'm sure you know what it's like having to juggle so much. Adam's great, you know, but he's no Richard. It'll take him a long time to step into his father's big shoes."

She caught a glimpse of Kate, who rolled her eyes emphatically. Colleen didn't need the song and dance, either.

"I'm doing my best to help out with the day-to-day operational stuff while he's learning, but that means letting some things slide."

"Mmm hmm." The Whitmans hadn't yet made a formal announcement about Adam's succession. The only reason Colleen knew was because someone at the tea farm told someone at Split Acres, who told Kate, who, in turn, told her.

"I've been trying to get a hold of you for weeks, and you've been so busy... "

"Busy would be an understatement."

"Hate to make it worse, but ... " He shifted his weight and cast his eyes toward the drop ceiling. "The column's due tomorrow morning for a Friday run."

She laughed. "In that case, no way. Thanks for the offer, but I've got too many plates in the air at the moment as it is."

"I totally understand. I don't know how you get as much done as you do, Colleen. But, listen. Let me give you the editor's card." Sam patted his pants pockets until he found his wallet in the front right one. He pulled it out and extracted one heavy stock card. On the back, using the wall as a support, he scribbled: Out of season produce.

"There ya go." He handed it to her. "That's the topic. If by some miracle you can find the time to type something up, send it straight to the editor, and he'll take care of everything from there."

"I don't know if I'll manage it, but thanks. I appreciate you thinking of me."

He waved a dismissive hand at her. "Aw, don't worry about it. I'd rather deal with you than your pop. You're much prettier."

She rolled her eyes but laughed. "Oh, get out of here."

"Bye, Colleen. Don't bust too many balls."

When the door closed behind him, Kate said, "I'm pretty sure he's included his in that group. You're the only woman I know who can make a fifty-eight-year-old man hem and haw."

"Not true," she said, skirting around the dog who'd returned and plopped himself onto the mat. She squeezed Kate's right shoulder on the way past the desk. "I learned half of my tricks from watching you."

CHAPTER TEN

Marriage was supposed to come with certain fringe benefits, including sharing a bed with one's spouse, and Alan went home after Colleen's farm tour mulling over ways to organize that feat. Before he could set his plan in motion, he figured he'd best share the news of his recent matrimony with Kimi. Her last email had been dripping with loneliness, and he figured some interesting news would cheer her up.

Oddly, she'd accepted his announcement with a small grunt and steered the conversation elsewhere. It was as if she didn't believe he'd do such a thing. Well, she was right if she thought that. Normally, he wouldn't.

"So, what's it like?" she asked. "Rainy?"

"Well ... " He slung his right leg up onto his rented sofa and loosened his bootlace knot. "Yes, it's pretty rainy here, but there's enough sun to keep me from wanting to pound my head against a wall."

"I'm surprised that of all places, you'd pick there. You've been all over the world. Why not a big city like New York or Washington, D.C.? Someplace where there's stuff to do and things to see."

"That's the difference between you and me, little sister. I didn't go wandering because I wanted to see great things. I wandered because I was trying to figure out where I should plant roots."

"And why there?"

"Hard to explain. Come visit. See for yourself."

"Really? I'm not sure I can manage it. I'm being watched like a hawk now that you've gone and thumbed your nose at our parents' carefully laid plans."

"I didn't, really. I didn't plan this. First, when I heard about the farm I thought it would be a good deal for the Prevost brand."

"Oh yes, our poor father very nearly had a stroke when he heard the news from his lawyer, or at least it looked like it with the way he foamed at the mouth. Right next to Emerald Tea. What luck, huh?"

"Yes, but, I've given this a lot of thought and I don't want the family involved in this. This may be my chance to have something for myself. Stop bobbing around and put down an anchor, so to speak."

"Right," she said blithely. "That's why you married ... wait, what's her name again, if she's even real?"

He pinched the bridge of his nose between his thumb and forefinger. "Colleen."

Colleen. Colleen who was *probably* at that exact moment having dinner with her ex-boss. While he'd been cleaning up the mess he'd made in her house with that final section of rewiring, she'd hurried past him dressed in a little black dress and sky-high silver heels and told him to lock up when he was done.

"Where are you going dressed like that at 1:00 P.M.?" he'd asked.

"First to a wrap party for the catalog and to celebrate me finishing that freelance work in record time then to Mancusos for dinner. They've got a killer spinach lasagna."

He groaned now even thinking of how tight that dress was and how it clung to her hips. Was a spike heel really necessary for a small-town Italian restaurant? Perhaps he should have encouraged her to take along a shawl. A long one. Perhaps one that reached the ground and wrapped all the way around her gorgeous body.

That newspaper wedding announcement from town hall couldn't come soon enough in his opinion. She may not have thought people were paying any attention to her, but they were. He'd seen it following her down Main Street to the municipal parking lot. The way supposedly decent men swiveled their necks as she walked past had ignited an unfamiliar rage in him.

"How do you know I hadn't been pining for her for ages and didn't marry her for love?" he asked Kimi, and bent to unknot his other boot.

"I'm sorry, I don't buy it. You're too picky for love, and you're not the kind of opportunist our brother is to marry her for any other reason. Prove to me she's real."

"For fuck's sake." He grunted, pulled his phone away from his ear, and worked the menus until he found the photo album. He selected the most recent image and sent it in a text.

Silence filled the line for a long while.

"You need a haircut," she said finally. "You got married looking like that?"

He said nothing, just heeled off his boots.

"Who took the picture?"

"Her secretary. It was the magistrate's idea. I guess that's what normal people do when they get married. Take pictures to commemorate the occasion."

"She doesn't look like your type. I thought you liked blondes."

That was because he'd never seen *Colleen*. "Doesn't matter what my type is or isn't. This is merely a business agreement."

She snorted. "Sure it is, and I'm merely wasting away on this farm because I'm too spoiled to work elsewhere."

They both laughed. Kimi's predicament was a long-standing joke between the two of them. She could get married and move away, but like Alan, she was under the same trust fund restrictions. Even if she found a guy willing to farm rooibos or pitch in at the winery, he'd have to pass the Prevost test.

Alan wasn't even sure he would pass it, and he was one.

If Kimi had her druthers, she'd have a big city life to go with her big city personality.

"In that picture, you're holding her like you mean it. There's no tension there. You're not that good an actor. She must be interesting."

"That she is."

"Good, so are you going to rescue me? Can you have a ticket waiting for me at the airport? Just tell me when."

"Running away from home isn't something mature women do."

"Oh, stop. You did it, and you were even younger."

"I'll try to get you out tonight if there's a flight. Be ready."

"I'll go pack."

"Bring your raincoat."

He disconnected and slumped lower in the sofa. Kimi had always had an unusual knack for reading him. She'd learned that skill quickly from the day she was adopted. Whether it was a coping tactic or just her way of adapting to her new and atypical surroundings, he couldn't say, but she was usually right.

Maybe he had held Colleen like he meant it, but he was a reasonable man and reasonable men knew they shouldn't hope for things they could never have.

His priorities hadn't changed. His most important consideration was securing the farm—a future for himself. If Colleen decided to stick around long after it ceased to be her burden, so much the better.

Actually, the idea was pretty bloody appealing. He'd always figured he'd marry some sweet, retiring woman who'd be the helpmate the Prevosts would expect in the family business, not some bulldog of a taskmaster who hated having to ask for aid.

He checked his watch. Thinking of the bulldog reminded him—he had a small task to take care of before bed. A little handyman work that couldn't wait, and it involved reconciling his new wife's address to his own.

•••

Weary to her bones, Colleen sank onto her bed and then even further as the lower left corner, then the right, dropped to the floor and the footboard fell in slow motion toward the dresser.

She rolled off the bedside, swearing under her breath, and rubbing her bruised hip. "Dammit! What now?"

Easing around to the foot of the bed, she knelt low and examined the faulty frame. Looked like a bolt was missing from one side, and there had been a very loose one on the other. She sighed and grabbed a pillow and blanket. Tired as she was, she didn't have the energy to fiddle around with it when a perfectly good couch called out to her.

Yeah, she'd overindulged a bit. The food had been so good, the conversation stimulating, and the wine kept coming. She hadn't been able to suppress her scoff when one of the bottles being passed around had the Prevost mark on it. Greg had teased her, asking if she'd become picky in the past couple of years. She'd chuckled and said she was simply remembering a joke from one of the staff members.

Big friggin' joke of a marriage.

Near the end of the meal, she'd wondered why she'd even left her job—her *life*—back in Seattle. Then she remembered because the reason never changed. She'd been born there at the farm, and it's where her heart was. Maybe Daddy wasn't in tune with the farm in the same way. He probably saw it as dirt and buildings and machines that could make him money, but she saw it as a living entity—something that had been on the losing end of a give and take relationship for too long.

One day, Colleen would set things right. The farm all her grandparents had invested so much into would be something people were proud to have in their community. At the moment, though, the only success she could claim was that she'd cancelled the daily newspaper delivery and slashed the staff down to bare bones.

She sighed and wriggled her body against the sofa cushions. She certainly wasn't going to get a pat on the back for that.

She needed to think big. *Bigger*. And to act bigger, but doing so would either get her disowned or struck from the will, not that there was anything left to squeeze out of *that*.

• • •

In the morning, she walked into the office, her back stiff and her brain in a fog.

Kate narrowed her eyes at her. "You look like what the cat dragged in, ate, and barfed up."

Colleen growled and cracked her back. "Bed fell apart last night. Slept on the sofa."

"Ooh!" Kate's eyes went round as saucers. "Were you doing anything fun?"

"Ha ha." If only she were. She'd rather wake up with a limp and a smile on her face than a stiff neck and sofa fabric indented on her cheeks. "Bed frame lost a couple bolts. Have you seen Alan yet? Maybe he's got a couple replacements in his truck."

"I've seen him, but—"

"Colleen!"

At the sound of her bellowed name, she closed her eyes and muttered, "Shit." She'd certainly heard that voice enough over the years to recognize it in a crowd of thousands.

Kate cringed. "Yeah. Your father is here and in your office. He wasn't due until tomorrow."

Colleen had been so busy, she'd forgotten Daddy was due in for that zoning board meeting. Worse, she needed to be there and hadn't prepared a damned thing. She and Alan needed to have a powwow ASAP.

"What's he doing in my office?"

"Besides waiting for you?"

Colleen groaned and ground the heels of her palms against her eyes. "Besides that."

"I think he was fishing around for some kind of paperwork. Better go see what he wants before the rest of the staff gets nosy."

"Yeah, they're good for that."

No sooner had Colleen turned her body toward the corridor when her father, red-faced and narrow-eyed, stormed down it with Arfer on his heels.

Standing three feet from her, he thrust a sheet of copy paper toward her and whisked his glasses off his nose. "Care to explain that?"

She swallowed and relaxed her facial muscles. She straightened her kinky spine and pushed her shoulders back. She took the paper and exhibited a false calm, locking her stare to her father's cold, gray gaze. "Good morning to you, too, Daddy."

"Right, where are my manners? Good morning, Colleen. Or should I say *Mrs. Prevost?*"

Whoops.

She cleared her throat and turned the paper around. Printed on the front was an automated e-mail sent to Daddy's personal e-mail account. The secretary of state's office notified him whenever there were changes to business documents filed with Washington. Scanning the terse document quickly, she raised her shoulders and handed it back.

"Good for them. They must be caught up on their paperwork in Olympia."

"What does it *mean*, Colleen?"

"Means I got married. Changed my name on a bunch of stuff. Sorry you and Mom weren't here for the wedding. It was magical. We had it between me monitoring the complete obliteration of yet another crop of potatoes and balancing the farm checking accounts down to the penny, which believe it or not, is very easy when there's no money coming in."

He blanched then shrugged. "That's farming for you. Things will pick up in the fall."

She shook her head, emphatically. "No. They won't. There's nothing here, Daddy, but a few bees and some apples and pears. Tomatoes are looking pretty anemic, so we can probably count those out for supermarket sales."

"What about the eggplants?"

"We may have enough eggplant this year to cover the cost of fuel."

"That's good. And what about the carrots and broccoli?"

She clucked her tongue and rolled her eyes toward the drop ceiling. "At the current viability rate, we'll be able to cover taxes."

"Well, that's good."

"*Late*. As usual. That is *not* good, Daddy. Just barely eking by isn't good enough. We're not subsistence farmers. This is a for-profit business. Have you forgotten that?"

He waved a dismissive hand. "We're in a recession. Things'll turn around. We'll plant some cabbage and garlic during the fall to make up for it."

"No, Daddy, that's not going to help. This farm has been bleeding money non-stop since you and Richard had it out. You had the cash back then to float the business and keep it in the black, but that nest egg is all dried up now. This farm is *not* self-supporting. You and Mom are out of living parents to tap for love offerings, and it's *not* going to turn around, recession or no recession, unless we take a serious look at our operations and make some drastic changes." Scraping a hand through the loose hair she hadn't had time to brush, she sighed. "And besides, a lot of our fields are far overdue for fallow time. They are *spent*, Daddy. Damn near barren. At the rate we're going, we won't even be able to grow moss. Right now? I'm Scarlett O'Hara and this place is Tara after the war, minus the radishes."

His eyes narrowed again. "So, what are you suggesting? Evidently you think I've run my own farm into the ground, so if you have better ideas, Miss Hotshot, I'd love to hear them."

"I believe that's *Missus* Hotshot."

Colleen hadn't heard the door open behind her, but there was another unmistakable voice. This one had a foreign accent and a deep, baritone rumble that made her cheeks burn hot.

Alan slipped an arm around her waist and drew her in for a short, but somehow incendiary kiss that set her libido on fire without even a hint of tongue.

Her knees buckled under her, just like that day in front of the magistrate, but he held her up, pressed against his side in the way husbands sometimes did. She wheezed. "Uh, hi."

"You were looking for me, Colleen?"

"Uh, yeah." She swallowed and finally met his tender gaze.

Damn good actor, he was.

"Was wondering if you could ... " *Wait, my husband technically lives with me. He'd know about the bed.* "Was wondering if you had any luck finding spare parts for the bed frame."

If the request perplexed him at all, he didn't show it. He just loosened his grip on her waist and shifted his tool belt so his hammer didn't stab her already bruised hip. "We may have to replace the whole thing. Needed a new bed, anyhow."

Daddy's eyes went round, and Colleen knew what he must have been thinking had befallen the old one.

If only.

"Last time I saw you," Daddy started, now leaning his butt against the edge of Kate's desk, "I'd hired you as a handyman. If I had known you and Colleen were dating ... "

"You would have what?" she prompted when he didn't seem likely to finish the statement. She didn't like the grin that crept across his face.

"I probably would have offered you more money. She's a handful. Has a mean swing with a softball bat, so watch out."

The polite grin Alan had been wearing broadened, and he shifted his gaze from Daddy to her.

She dared him with her glare.

She dared him to say something stupid, something chauvinist.

His eyes flitted downward to the hand on her left hip, and he cocked up an eyebrow. "Did you lose your ring already, sweetheart?"

Her ring?

She brought her left hand in front of her face and groaned again. Dammit, she'd taken the ring off before dinner because she wasn't ready for the barrage of questions that would surely come from Greg and her old coworkers. Where had she put it after dinner? She was pretty sure she'd put it back on after putting on her … Ah. She hadn't slept in pajamas. The ring was probably at the bottom of the laundry basket with the cocktail dress that had made her feel like an encased sausage all evening.

"I took it off this morning before I went up to that overgrown flower field by the visitor entrance." It used to be a manicured picnic area, but the flowers took over… which wasn't such a bad thing since some of them were native and heirloom and could be making Split Acres some money if they were cultivated in a controlled environment. "Was checking those yellow irises for seed pods. Didn't finish. Only eyed about a quarter of them." That gave her some wiggle room to actually go *do* the job.

"Oh, honey," Kate said with a dismissive flick of her hand. "Down South where I'm from, the ladies think fresh dirt from gardening adds a little something to the quality of gold, and the diamonds, too. Or maybe it's the other way around—the contact from the diamonds adds a little something special to their compost. Ladies had some beautiful gardens, too."

Well, Colleen didn't have a diamond to worry about. Just a narrow band she imagined was popular with the shotgun wedding set.

"Don't worry about getting your ring scuffed up," Alan said in an unusually flat voice. When she turned to look at him, his expression was unreadable. "They're meant to get a bit scraped, just like marriages. If they're too pristine, they likely symbolize a very tenuous relationship."

Ouch.

"Didn't realize you were a philosopher in addition to a handyman," Daddy said with a chuckle. He pulled a little paper cup from the wall-mounted dispenser and filled it with water from the cooler she had been on the fence about sending back to the company. The staff could get their water from the sink, just like she did.

"Jack of all trades," Alan mumbled. He closed in the small distance between them and took her left hand into his. Bringing it to his lips, he kissed the back, locking an intense blue stare on her.

What had gotten into him this morning?

He let the hand fall gently and turned on his boot heel toward the door. "I'll try to fix the bed, but it may be a lost cause."

Before he could slip out, she drew him back and put her lips against his ear, "We need to talk." She gave his bicep a little admiring squeeze before her brain caught on to what her hands were doing. She didn't want to transmit the wrong idea, but what would that be? That she was attracted to him, or that she wanted him to *know* she found him attractive?

Her head swam.

He brushed his lips against her ear and whispered back, "About what?"

How he'd managed to make a simple three-syllable question sound like a sexual suggestion, she had no clue. She sucked in some air.

"Zoning meeting. Daddy doesn't know we're presenting."

"Dinner at the diner, then." He nodded and slipped through the door.

She glanced at Kate, who barely brought her newspaper in front of her face right as her shoulders began to shake with laughter.

Daddy strode over, sipping his ice-cold water and knitting his thick, gray eyebrows together with concentration. "The meeting? Why would he want to be witness to that? It'll be like watching paint dry, or even better—tea grow." He laughed at his own little joke, but she didn't think it was funny.

She stepped over Arfer, like it was just an ordinary day and locked herself into her office.

Tapping her forehead a few times against her desktop, she muttered, "This is a train wreck in the making, and I'm co-conductor."

And then her chair collapsed beneath her.

CHAPTER ELEVEN

Alan hadn't expected to feel so pissed about something as superficial as a cheap gold band, but seeing Colleen not wearing hers had triggered some land mine in him he hadn't known was there. He hadn't thought about what that ring meant to other people until she'd decided not to wear it.

Why did she really take it off? And why was he so mad?

Maybe that was a dumb question. He knew why he was mad. He had this gorgeous prize of a wife, and even if their marriage was just a business arrangement, while they were wed, he wanted the world to know Colleen Sanders was off-limits. Maybe pride was rearing its ugly head, but he didn't care. Colleen was his.

Until she wasn't.

"That's a Colleen face if I've ever seen one," Pixie said as she set two ceramic mugs on the table. "She must be rubbing off on you. You're thinking too hard."

"Yes, I think I am." He looked out the large window to his right and watched his tardy wife jump down from her truck with her computer bag.

Pixie filled each cup to the brim with coffee. "How's the honeymoon?"

"Ha, ha."

"Let me give you some advice about Colleen from an old teacher's perspective." Pixie pressed her palms onto the tabletop and raised her eyebrows, waiting for the go-ahead.

He cut his gaze to the parking lot once more to see Colleen struggling to close the driver's door. It kept bouncing back. Latch must have been broken. "All right. Let me have it."

"Have you met Rebecca?"

"Colleen's mother? No. She hasn't been around."

"Yeah, she's been looking for an excuse to hide ever since Sheila Whitman died. She couldn't grieve in peace around here. Even after the farms split, they were best friends. Used to come here to eat together when they didn't want to be seen. Joe would have gotten on her case about it. Anyway, they'd bring Colleen with them sometimes. I guess she would have been around middle school age."

Alan checked the window again. Colleen had put down the bag and was peering at the door lock mechanism. Normally, he'd go help, but he needed this insight from Pixie.

"Colleen never said anything to Joe about the meetings, but around age fourteen or so, she'd stopped coming."

"Why?"

"That, I can only speculate on, but that was the year at the State Fair that some insensitive asshole looked at her name placard under some produce she was showing, and said, 'Oh, Split Acres. Isn't that one of the Whitman brands?' To put the cherry on top of that ice cream sundae of an event, she lost the blue ribbon to Adam, and second place to his brother Daniel. In the scheme of things, third place was an excellent showing. That was third in the *state*, but then the local newspaper photographer couldn't find her at the event, so, in the paper the next day… "

"It was just the Whitmans."

She nodded. "I think she's been a surprisingly good sport about most things, but after a while, I bet it all starts to feel like a pile-on."

They turned at the sound of a thump and saw Colleen waving a triumphant fist in the air. She'd gotten the damned thing closed.

Alan grinned.

"Listen," Pixie said, picking up her coffee decanter. "I'd bet she feels really naked. People know too much about her and about Split Acres. It's good that you were a stranger. I'll be back to get your orders." She squeezed his shoulder and walked to the kitchen.

Colleen slid into the opposite side of the booth, grumbling. "What's going to fall apart on me next?" She opened her bag and extracted a thick manila folder.

"If I had to guess, I'd say one of those chairs in your office."

Her lip twitched at the corner, but otherwise, she gave nothing away. She wouldn't tell him about the chair, but naturally he already knew. He was the one who'd pulled the spindly thing's life support.

"Colleen, please tell me what you need, and I'll get it for you."

She fondled the corner of the folder and looked absently out the window. "That's okay."

There she went again, refusing to ask for help that he was pretty much begging to give her.

He didn't know why he was so concerned with the woman's comfort because it was in direct opposition to his goal: edging her out of the farm. Kitting her out with a plush office wouldn't make her more likely to sign over the land and business.

Pixie came back with her pad. "The usual, Colleen?"

"Yeah."

"Alan?"

"I'll have what she's having."

Colleen raised an eyebrow. "You don't even know what I'm having."

"You have good taste, marrying me aside. I trust you."

She opened her mouth as if to rebut, then closed it. Whatever snide remark she was going to make, she tamped down.

That was progress, wasn't it?

"You won't be disappointed, Alan," Pixie said, and she walked away.

"Tell me what to expect tomorrow. I haven't had the privilege of witnessing the Emerald Springs government in action."

Colleen pushed some loose hair behind her ear and sighed. "I haven't been to one of these in a really long time myself, so I'm hoping they didn't change the order of business. I really want to get in and get out because I suspect when people put two and two together about who you are, the rumor mill will be working on overdrive. People are probably going to think we're pointing our guns at Emerald Tea, and who could blame them?"

"Hmm." Alan leaned back and rubbed his jaw. Maybe a little healthy fear was better than pity. Split Acres could be a force to be reckoned with, especially with plans like Colleen's. She understood her father's obsession with tradition, but her creativity helped her picture ways to adapt what was already there to make a healthier, more functional business. Joe was an idiot for not listening. "Perhaps I shouldn't go. If I'm not there, that'll give you some more time to set plans in motion without the suspicious backlash."

"I thought about that, and was going to suggest it, but then I thought about Daddy."

"What about him?"

"For an average-sized man, he has an ego the size of a blue whale. If I offer a suggestion, most of the time he systematically vetoes it because apparently I haven't *really* thought things through and, you know, all that estrogen makes me say silly things."

"He said that?" Wanting to punch his father-in-law in the nose probably wasn't a good thing. Did Joe know his daughter at all? He must not have, or he would have known how bright she was and how observant she was about the way the farm ticked. He would have gotten out of her way to let her *work* if he knew her.

"He implied it," she said softly. "I hate having to lean on you to say things to him and the zoning board I can say myself, but if you're there, I suspect Daddy will actually listen before he says no. I just need him to listen."

"Tell me what to do, and I'll do it."

"Great." She leaned back as Pixie slid a BLT on whole wheat under her nose.

"See, I knew you had good taste."

She managed a tiny grin.

He thanked Pixie for his meal, and when she'd walked away, he unrolled his napkin and stared at Colleen's left hand. "Do you need help finding your ring?"

She looked down at her fingers as if she'd forgotten there was supposed to be jewelry there. "Oh." She dropped her hand onto her lap. "No. I know where it is. I'll dig it out before the meeting tomorrow."

He didn't respond. He just picked up his sandwich and bit into it because really, the ring meant nothing. His trust fund disbursement didn't depend on it. Maybe that ring was his way of calling dibs on her even though he knew he couldn't keep her.

That didn't seem like a business arrangement to him.

That seemed personal.

• • •

The following afternoon, he watched the doors at SeaTac for his little sister. Airport police was trying to keep the traffic moving, but he'd already circled around three times so they'd have to just suck it up. Kimi was inexperienced with international travel, and here she was, flying all the way to United States with only a couple hours' notice. Adventurous, that girl was.

He scoffed and eyed the rearview mirror for signs of the Segway-riding cop. "Girl. Ha." Kimi was a grown woman and had been grown for seven years now. Twenty-five seemed a long way back for him.

Wow, thirty-five. When'd that happen?

What had he been doing in all those years since leaving South Africa? They'd begun to blur. That couldn't be good. Maybe the best he thing could do for himself was to put down some roots, and right now, any place was probably as good as another. He simply *preferred* to be where he was.

He liked Emerald Springs and the town's unostentatious charm. Sure, initially he'd stuck around because he wanted a shot at a position at the tea farm, but now he knew he'd probably stay awhile even without employment.

Employment. The thing he actually didn't need, given the sudden inflation of his savings account that the marriage kicked in. He could probably buy himself a small island and steal Colleen away from her beloved patch of dirt to keep him company.

He grinned at the thought. Some company. She'd just as soon scratch his eyes out with her wedding ring.

The airport police officer tapped on his passenger side window at the same time Kimi exploded through the automated doors with her mounds of luggage in the care of a skycap.

Now he laughed outright and waved the kind policeman away. "I'm waiting for her," he mouthed, pointing to the approaching princess.

She beamed as she walked closer, and even without the windows being rolled down, Alan could hear her little squeals.

He jumped down from the driver's seat, gave his little sister a crushing hug that lifted her several inches off the ground, then set her on her feet. "You're looking very cheerful following twenty-eight hours of travel, Kimi." He wrapped his fingers around one of her larger bag's handles and heaved the suitcase into his cargo bed. "And why do you have so much luggage?"

"Well." She rooted through her purse, drew out a wadded handful of colorful bills and furrowed her forehead at it.

"I'll take care of it." He gave the skycap twenty bucks and thanked him for hauling what had to be Kimi's entire wardrobe out to the curb. Unlike her big brother, she didn't travel light.

"Of course I'm cheerful. I'm somewhere that isn't home!" She clapped her hands and did a little bounce. "And regarding the luggage, well … " She raised her shoulders in a shrug and moved toward the passenger door.

Alan raised the tailgate and joined her at the front seat.

She continued, "I figured I'd do some exploring while I'm here, and I didn't know how long I'd stay."

"I see." He eased into the flow of traffic, and once he was on the highway heading toward the valley, he stole a glance away from the road and watched Kimi staring with great interest at the passing countryside. He hated to disturb her reverie, but he had to ask. "Do our parents know you left?"

"No."

"Really? You managed to sneak out of the complex with all that luggage? Who helped you?"

"Fritz."

"Ah." Fritz was a good guy. He'd play dumb if the Prevosts asked questions.

"Yeah. He drove me to the airport and told me to give you all the birthday punches he owed you."

He laughed. "Hasn't been that long since I was last there."

"Five years, Alan. That's one hundred and sixty-five punches plus five for luck."

"I bet Fritz had a great time doing that math."

"He did. Made his head hurt. Said he used to make birthday punches a training tool back when he was still coaching boxers. If he managed to land any blows, he'd add another."

"Ouch." He and Fritz were the best of friends until Alan left. In fact, his buddy had driven him to the airport all those years ago, too.

"So, I guess you're a rich man now."

"You don't hash your words. Never stop being you, Kimi."

She put up her hands palms out in a conciliatory gesture. "I'm just wondering what you're going to do with yourself is all."

"You know I'll always find a way to keep busy. What's that saying? Idle hands are the devil's tools?"

"That's right. Are you really going to stay put, or are you itching to wander some more?" She twirled the ends of several of her long braids around her index finger and really studied him, awaiting his response.

"I'd like to stay put."

"For the farm, right?"

"Naturally."

"Mmm hmm. I bet you don't even want to grow tea."

He checked his mirror and eased over to the right lane. "You're right. I don't want to compete with the Whitmans, and I don't want the Prevost legacy propping me up."

"Ah. You're going to do this the hard way, are you?"

"When have I ever taken the easy route to anything?"

She raised one shoulder and let it fall, grinning broadly so her perfect white teeth set off her rosy brown skin. "And this Colleen, what does she have to say about your world domination strategy?"

"Let me conquer the farm first, then I'll worry about the world," he said with a chuckle. "There's a meeting tonight I need to be at. Need to discuss some zoning issues the community would have to weigh in on, and that's where I'm going right after I drop you off at the inn."

"Inn?" She pulled back the foil on a very large bar of dark chocolate and took a nip off the corner. "I thought I'd stay at your place."

"Yes, well, unfortunately Colleen has had some issues with her furniture and will probably need someplace to sleep. I thought I'd offer her my bed." He was probably paving his own road to Hell for what he'd done to that woman's bed. Oh, and that pipe under her hot water heater. By the time the leak did its job, she'd not only need a new subfloor, but that old ugly tile in the kitchen would need replacing. Maybe she'd even thank him for it later.

Much later, probably.

"Oh, I see," Kimi said with a purr.

He looked over to find her wriggling her dark eyebrows.

"Sneaky boy. Didn't think you had skullduggery in your impressively diverse repertoire of tricks."

"She brings it out of me. She's ... "

She was what? Some sort of witch who had him under a spell that seemed more intricate, more unbreakable each day?

Kimi just nodded. She always knew. He didn't have to say a word. "I can't wait to meet her."

• • •

Colleen wrenched her hands, pacing in front of City Hall. Where was Alan? Perhaps in the future, they'd do better if they communicated in person rather than relying on text messages. They had the podium in about fifteen minutes, and he was nowhere to be seen.

"Dammit." She stood on tiptoes, scanning over the tops of cars in the lot in search of his pickup truck. Daddy was already inside, but he had no idea the Sanderses had an item on the zoning discussion agenda. He never looked at the damned agenda, actually. Most of what he did during these local government events was schmooze and bolster his constituency base. He planned to run again at the end of his term, and he needed to appear *concerned* and whatnot.

"There he is." She blew out a relieved breath and stepped down the curb, heading toward the back of the lot.

The passenger-side door opened first, and she paused.

Who was in his truck? Kate, maybe? Though she couldn't fathom why Kate would be interested in boring zoning issues when she could be at home watching *Jeopardy!*

A woman hopped down—a small, elegant woman who had the kind of beauty that seemed to intensify the longer a person stared. Her garments were simple—dark jeans, a white tank, and a drapey, gray wrap slung artfully over her shoulders—but obviously high quality. The giant leather purse she pulled down from the seat had likely cost more than Colleen's last root canal.

The woman pushed a pair of large, round sunglasses onto the top of her braided hair and scanned the parking lot and town surrounding it with a curious grin on her face.

Colleen didn't know her, but knew she wasn't a local.

Now Alan came around, oblivious to anything but the elegant, little woman, and when he reached her, he wrapped his arms around her waist and drew her up into a hug that lifted her feet off the ground.

Heart pounding, Colleen took a step forward to ... well, she didn't know what she was going to do. Yell? For what? For him not being discreet about his side flings? She couldn't rightfully get angry about him seeking attention elsewhere, but couldn't he at least not embarrass her publicly?

Now he kissed the woman's forehead and set her down. He reached into the back pocket of his slacks, fished out his wallet, and opened the billfold.

The woman accepted the cash he offered, and walked away with a wave.

Alan shrugged and replaced his wallet.

Colleen tucked her tube of blueprints under her arm, propped her free fist on her hip and walked with purpose to the truck. He had the audacity to hold a hand out toward her as he approached, and she paused, staring at it briefly with some malice, but took it when churning gravel behind her indicated they had an audience. He may have forgotten about their united front, but she hadn't.

She took his hand and wrapped it around her elbow, already angling them toward the building. "We're on the agenda in ten minutes. Daddy is holding seats for us." Alan looked good in slacks. Flat-front, navy blue, and well-fitted. Who needed porn when there were men like him who looked so damned good with a shirt tucked in and a shiny belt buckle? And the way he rolled his dress shirt's sleeves up to just beneath his elbows to show off his strong forearms …

She'd always fallen for men with athletic builds, so she shouldn't have been surprised at her arousal. She was more surprised she hadn't been able to compartmentalize that part of their relationship. He was just the funds of the operation. The sex was a one-time thing, and …

Oh, he combed his hair.

She squelched a squeal, and turned away, giving her brain an imaginary cold shower by thinking about her IRA balance.

She said nothing until they'd climbed the thirteen steps at the front of the building and approached the revolving door. "We're coming in late, so most of the tedium has already been hashed out. They put me on the agenda early, so we don't have to wait around too long."

"Are they going to vote on it today?"

"No." She waved at the security officer at the front desk and grinned when he looked curiously at her familiarity with Alan. She didn't answer the guard's unasked question, and just signed them in and took the badges he pushed across the countertop.

"There's a cooling-off period," she said as she led Alan down the left-most corridor. "That's what I call it, anyway. Basically, you introduce your discussion item, anyone who has an objection to it can voice it, the officials put it on the record, they send some minions out to your business to assess the environmental impact and such, and then you get a decision in the mail shortly after."

"Why would they even care? You're so far out."

"Still in the city limits, but you wouldn't think so because we get no city services. We even haul our own trash."

She pulled open the heavy swinging door and ignored the stares of the folks seated in the back rows. She pulled Alan up the aisle and joined Daddy in the second row, near the outer edge.

Daddy ended his whispered conversation with the Ford dealership owner and acknowledged them with a nod. "Your mother drove down to meet Alan, I guess. She said she didn't want to go out anywhere, but she cooked. We need to pick up dessert."

Sure thing. Right after you pick your jaw up off the floor.

One of the stuffy talking heads seated on the front dais said into his mic, "Coming up next, we have a zoning item from Split Acres Farm. Will your representative please step up to mic two?"

"Wait, did he say Split Acres?" Daddy mused. "That can't be right. Must be some mistake."

Colleen reached across Alan's lap and patted Daddy's knee. "I submitted it, Daddy," she whispered. "Just sit here and pretend you know what's going on. Hold your bellowing until later because it'll all be moot if we don't get zoning approval."

"But—"

"*Later*, Daddy." She uncapped the tube of blueprints and slipped the collated stack of documents Kate had prepared that morning out of her bag.

Alan followed her up the aisle and took a place at the microphone while Colleen distributed paperwork to the men in cheap suits. He started, "Gentlemen, we submitted copies of these to the zoning office this morning for filing per regulations. I understand this should be fairly cut and dried."

"Please state your name for the record and your affiliation to Split Acres Farm," the same bureaucrat from before asked.

"Apologies. My name is Alan Prevost, and I'm married to Colleen Prevost, neé Sanders. Colleen and I...run the farm in the senator's absence."

She cringed, though no one saw it because they were all watching Alan. *Probably should have had an answer prepared for that in advance.*

A whispered buzz erupted in the room, and she could catch only snatches of it. Some of it seemed to be the expected, *When did Colleen get married?* and the rest was, *What did he say his name was?*

The bureaucrat cleared his throat and murmured, "Please continue."

Colleen settled next to Alan at the podium, and tuned him out as she scanned the room for reactions.

Maybe this was a bad idea. Maybe I should have done the talking, and that way no one would know about Alan. It had seemed a good idea at the time—for them to have a united front so Daddy wouldn't dismiss her ideas so quickly. He'd always see her as his little girl, no matter how intelligent, how competent she was. Alan was an outsider, and one from a family renowned for making remarkably savvy business decisions.

She tuned back in as one of the men in suits asked, "So, to be clear for the sake of the folks in audience, you're shifting some of your commercial farming activities into greenhouses, and need zoning permission to engage in light manufacturing of refined goods on-site. You're adding..." He pushed his reading glasses up and squinted at the documents. "Three new buildings?"

"Um ... " She leaned into the mic. "Four, counting the farm store, so that complicates things. We've never engaged in manufacturing or on-site sales before. Right now, we're just zoned for farming."

Alan eased out of the way and let her have the mic.

"We're moving away from farm-to-consumer sales and what commercial farming we do at this point will be under contract for large buyers. We're expanding our floral yields and our honey production and we'll sell those products, in addition to dried fruits, in the farm shore. No crops."

She stole a look at her dad, who sat with his fingers threaded atop his thighs. His expression was a practiced blank, which not only meant he was short on words, but also incensed. She needed him short on words. If he didn't talk, he wouldn't mess this up for them. She hoped he understood that.

"Yes, Mr. Whitman, you're acknowledged. Please step up to microphone one," the moderator said.

Adam Whitman eased out of his mid-row seat near the right side of the room and approached the mic stand.

"Yes, my name is Adam Whitman, and I speak on behalf of Emerald Tea Farm. My concern with these plans, which I haven't heard of before this evening by the way, is the potential impact on our organic operations. I need to know if we need a wider barrier between our properties so we can avoid cross-pollination from the added bee population and—"

Colleen sighed and cut him off. "I'm sorry, Adam. You have the right to be concerned; however, if you'd take a look at our crop list, you'll see none of ours will cross-pollinate with any of yours, aside from the fruit. Further, I'd venture to say our orchards are far enough away from yours that you won't have any more issues with seed-spreading than from what birds and other critters are already doing for us."

Adam opened his mouth to rebut something, but she cut him off again. She wasn't in the mood to be cheerfully patient. What little patience she had had been sloughed off in the parking lot when another woman had debarked her so-called *beloved*'s vehicle.

"Mr. Whitman, if we came down here to niggle over every little change that occurred at the tea farm that could potentially affect Split Acres in some small way, of which there have been many, we'd have you tied up in so much red tape, you'd all asphyxiate."

"I'm just looking out for the best interests of my family's farm, Colleen."

"And that's exactly what I'm doing, *Adam*. I—*we*—are working to position our farm so that it is profitable and sustainable in the long-term. You shouldn't see that as a personal slight. You've certainly had enough construction over at the Emerald Tea you never ran past us, and we didn't complain. Not even when you poured that new roadway leading back to your pumpkin fields, and one of the workers backed his truck over our irrigation pipe. We didn't gripe. We just fixed it, because it wasn't worth making a big deal of. And when you have that Farm Fest every fall and people decide to park on our property because you don't have overflow, we don't whine when their vehicles leave deep ruts in our fields and disturb our garlic. We don't send them away."

"You should have said something. We would have reimbursed your farm for the—"

The zoning chief pounded his gavel on his bench. "You two can hash out your differences off the record … or in the newspaper again, if you can coordinate it."

She rolled her eyes. If she had known she and Adam would be sharing column space, she wouldn't have scrambled to get that article in as a favor for Sam. Naturally, they'd taken oppositional views on the subject, and even though they hadn't directly addressed each other in their contributions, they came across as confrontational. *Exactly* what she needed—for folks to think she was stoking the flames of the fire her father and Richard had started, especially now that her new last name could be construed as a threat.

"If there are no other objections to the proposed zoning changes for Split Acres, we'll move on to the next item."

She scanned the room, studied Daddy's now placid expression briefly, assessed the amusement from the folks in the peanut gallery, and let her gaze flit back to Adam, who looked perturbed.

Good. Let him be.

She always gave as good as she got, though, and locked her features into her *hell in high heels* expression.

Adam looked away.

"No further objections, then? Thank you, Split Acres. Mr. Whitman, we'll keep your complaint in mind as we assess the plan in the coming week."

"Thank you," Alan said into the mic.

Colleen grabbed her husband's hand, and pulled him down the aisle, past Daddy, past all the spectators, and didn't stop until they were safely in the lobby.

Or maybe *not* so safe. From the second set of doors came Adam with his younger brother Daniel on his heels.

"God," she murmured. She let go of Alan's hand, and walked to the security station. She unpinned her badge as the Whitmans drew nearer.

"Colleen," Adam started. "I think we need to sit down and hash some things out. I think there are a lot of ... " He cast his blue-green gaze toward Alan, who crossed his arms over his chest impassively. Adam cleared his throat. "I think we have a lot of misunderstandings that merit discussion."

She signed herself and Alan out and pushed a strand of errant hair out of her eyes. God, why had she worn these heels? Her arches were screaming from the abuse. She hadn't worn this particular pair in two years, at least, but every time she had, she'd gotten what she wanted. Men in suits had always been easy to sway with a sharp tongue and spike heel.

Alan chimed in, "Gentlemen, we have an appointment this evening. Perhaps call Kate at the farm on Monday, and we'll meet with you the next time Joe is available?"

Adam seemed to not have heard him and just stared.

Daniel said, "I'd heard you got married, but I didn't know ... "

"Good evening, gentleman." Alan gave Colleen's hand a little yank, and she followed him to his truck, although she'd driven herself.

They shut the doors and watched the rearview mirrors until the Whitmans dispersed. When they'd driven away, Colleen put her hand on the door handle and pulled.

Alan reached across her body and grabbed the bar, preventing her exit. "Hey. We should wait for your father," he said.

She closed her eyes and counted slowly in her head to ten, trying very hard not to be distracted by the press of his arm against her belly, or the warmth of his breath along the stretch of exposed skin at her collar. She opened her eyes and met his gaze.

That gaze that always made her words scramble in her head and her heart race.

"I need to go," she said. "I've got to pay some long-overdue bills right after I rustle up a new desk chair."

He let go of the handle and nodded.

Just that simple, and he'd acquiesced? But of course he would. He had a hot date waiting. One that was probably more his type—sweet and cute, two things Colleen hadn't been since she was ten. That had been when a little boy gave her a playful cuff on the playground, and she'd given him a black eye in return. Poor Adam. Fortunately, the school system kept them out of the same classes until ninth grade after that, and she'd learned to take her anger out on the field hockey pitch.

"See you on Monday, or whenever," she said, slamming the door.

He started his truck engine, and backing out of his space, he rolled down the window and said, "Right. Monday. Maybe you'll wear those shoes to the office."

She growled as he motored away.

CHAPTER TWELVE

Later that evening at his apartment, Alan set down his fork and pulled his cell phone across the coffee table as Kimi turned down his television volume.

He grinned as he read the digital display. "Hi, Colleen," he answered.

She sighed on her end. "I've got a little problem at the house."

"What happened?"

"There's a leak somewhere. Half the house is flooded. I would call a plumber, but … "

"Right. I'll come take a look. Be there in fifteen minutes."

"See ya."

He ended the call and set his phone back on the table. He grabbed his fork and his plate of chicken tikka and dug back in.

He felt Kimi's hard stare on the side of his face. No need to look up, so he kept eating.

"Well?" she asked.

"Well *what?*"

"You're just going to leave her waiting?"

"I'm just going to finish my dinner. Thank you, by the way, for picking that up."

"It was a cute little restaurant. The owner is from Kolkata via Manchester. We had a great discussion about the state of football."

"You don't know anything about football."

"He did most of the talking. I just kept shoveling rice into my mouth."

"Have our parents tried phoning you yet?"

"Hmm." She untangled her legs from beneath her rump and fetched the purse hanging on his apartment's door's knob. She slipped the phone out of the front pocket, and pressed the power button. After a moment, she said, "Yes, apparently." She returned the phone to the bag.

"Aren't you going to listen?"

"Not right now."

"Kimi, they might report you missing to the police or something. I can imagine the headlines: Prevost Tea Princess Missing. Kidnappers to Blame."

She waved a dismissive hand at him. "I left a note. Should have found it by now."

"What did the note say?"

She didn't answer, just turned up the television volume.

Twenty minutes later, he stopped his truck in front of Colleen's house and hopped out. She was on the porch, changed out of that clingy blue dress she'd been wearing at the zoning board session, and in her usual all black gear and rubber boots.

Pity. That scripture about people hiding their light under bushels came to mind.

He made a big show of walking back to his truck to fetch his toolbox before acknowledging her. "So, tell me what happened?"

She took her feet off the porch rail and pulled herself to standing. "I think it's the hot water heater. One of those old pipes rusted through."

"Oh, what a mess." He couldn't even feel bad about it. The damned water heater was probably as old as her truck. She needed a new one, and new pipes besides, and he was happy to give them to her. He'd decided that even if he took the farm, she could keep her little house. Maybe she'd even stay on in her current job while he handled the actual *farming* component of the business.

He shook his head at the thought. Yeah right. There he went again, calling dibs and trying to keep her for himself as if she'd really have him.

She followed him all the way to the utility closet, standing back a few feet to give him room to wrench the knob off.

"Sorry about the floors," he said. "They're probably ruined, but we can leave a few windows open tonight to air it out in here a bit. I'll get up what I can with the shop vac."

She sighed. "You know, I've always hated this little house and the idea of pumping money into it to fix it up chafes me."

He stilled for a moment, surprised, then patted his hands dry on his jeans and stood. "Why do you hate it?"

"Long story, and I don't want to sound sentimental."

"Tell me." He closed the closet door and followed her to the cellar to fetch the shop vac.

He plugged it in, but didn't turn it on. Instead, he just watched her watch him. Finally, she gave up waiting, and threw up her hands.

"Okay. When my father and Richard started WhitSand Farm decades ago, there were a few families who lived on this stretch of land—what's now ours and also where the Whitmans are currently—who were sort of in the way of the expansion. They were just little family farms and couldn't really compete, so Daddy and Richard bought them out. Those families moved away—to where, I don't know. When I was a kid, maybe around ten, I asked my mom whose house this was. No one had lived in it for as long as I could remember, and she told me it was no one's—that it was just a part of the farm and maybe one day we'd do something with it. We were living in the new house by then, but I couldn't help being so damned curious."

"Go on."

"All right. One day, me and Jacob were riding the four wheelers around, and decided to sneak a peek inside the house. He jimmied the cellar door open—you wouldn't know he's a cop now, right?— and we got our flashlights and looked around." Her lips pressed into a tight line, and she shook her head.

"What?"

"It was ... eerie. It was like the folks who lived here hadn't even had warning they were going to move. There was a lot of furniture left behind, some toys. Clothes." She swallowed. "Pictures."

"Did you ask your parents about it?"

"Daddy refused to talk about it, but Mom told me the family fought the move. Their property had been in foreclosure, and the sheriff had to see them off the property. She yelled at me for coming here without permission, then she got really sad and said she didn't know where the people had gone or what to do with their stuff."

"Where is the stuff?"

She bobbed her head toward the west. "In that old shed with the padlock. Mom put all the pictures into plastic totes so they wouldn't get destroyed by the weather, but I'm sure everything else out there needs to be trashed."

"I could see where that would put a bad taste in your mouth." Hell, with Split Acres in the state it was, it could have been the Sanderses abandoning their possessions and walking away from a farm they couldn't keep. Here he was, thinking he'd fix the place up for her, and the truth was it wasn't the house's disrepair she was so disenchanted about, but the condition on which the house came to them. That changed things. It was her damned guilt again, and yet again; she'd inherited the guilt her father should have been feeling. If he'd felt it the way she did, he would have acted on it. Alan sure would have.

"Why don't you just leave it?" he asked softly.

"And go where?"

"What about your parents' house?"

"You're thirty-five. Would you enjoy the prospect of living under your parents' roof when you've been on your own all this time?"

"I see your point." He didn't want to state the obvious just yet. "How about into an apartment in town?"

Finally, she cracked a grin. "I'd just as soon get myself a mobile home and park it behind the office. You said it yourself—my truck is unreliable and will probably die soon. Can you believe I traded a newish BMW in for that thing? What a sucker I am."

He returned her grin and pulled the shop vac closer to the utility closet. "I'm sure it was very charming on the lot. But, you don't have to buy a trailer, Colleen. You could stay with me. I did suggest it earlier this week."

"Stay with *you*?"

Leaning his back against the closet door, he shrugged and met her cautious stare. "It would hardly be irregular. We *are* married, in case you've forgotten."

"I haven't forgotten, but evidently you have."

"What are you talking about?"

"Don't play dumb. The woman in your truck earlier? Pretty as a painting and very affectionate?"

He laughed. At no point had he thought Colleen would construe his affection to Kimi as anything but familial or else he would have rushed to make an introduction. He'd chosen not to there in the parking lot because Kimi had a habit of subtly offending people she didn't like, and he feared she wouldn't like Colleen.

"The tiny woman with braids, you mean?"

She shrugged.

"Yes, she is pretty. I worry about that a lot, especially since I never go home. I always fear she'll hook up with the wrong sort. Get taken advantage of." He switched on the vacuum and pointed the hose toward the closet corner.

"So, she's from home?" Colleen shouted over the din.

"Yes. She's my sister. *Kimi*."

"Your sister?"

"Adopted, obviously, but very much loved."

"Uh … can you turn that thing off?"

He hit the switch and raised an eyebrow at her. Jealous? Colleen?

She blew out a breath and rubbed her eyes. "I'm sorry. I didn't know you had family in town."

"Kimi flew in this afternoon. Spur-of-the-moment thing."

"Oh. Hey, let me worry about the water. If I had known you were preoccupied, I would have just handled it myself. You don't have to—" She reached for the hose, but he stopped her, grabbed her wrists, and drew her close to him.

Before she could take a step away, he wound his arm around her waist and pressed her more fully against his front. She cast a wary gaze up at him, lips parted, eyes narrowed. "There's no one watching. You don't have to pretend to like me."

"Who's pretending?"

"Let me go," she whispered, and her voice was so pleading that he did it, though he hated to. She fit right there, pressed against him. Her moving in the opposite direction seemed unnatural.

He switched the vacuum back on and said over the noise, "Why don't you get a couple of days of clothing? I promise, I won't molest you in your sleep. You can take my bedroom, and I'll sleep on the sofa."

"You sure?"

"Yeah." He shut the closet door and moved the vacuum canister toward the soggy bedroom. "It'll be good for public opinion if you're seen coming out of my place, don't you think? And we could carpool to the farm. Just give me thirty minutes." He indicated the shop vac.

She nodded, turned on the heel of her rubber boot, and sloshed into her bedroom.

Lying to her was getting harder with each passing day. That's what made him so different from his parents. He didn't want to manipulate people to get what he wanted, and if that meant he wouldn't get it … so be it.

CHAPTER THIRTEEN

Alan carried her overnight bag up the stairs of his two-story walk-up. His apartment was situated over the pharmacy, and she'd always assumed that second level was merely a false front. She'd never had reason to go into the back lot.

"Wow," she said as he pushed the door open. The loft was huge, airy, and surprisingly modern with its open beam ceiling and bright track lights. "You rent this?"

He shrugged and set her bag atop the kitchen counter. "Rent to own, actually. Nobody else wanted it, so the owner wrote in that provision to the lease just in case I decided to stick around."

"Are you kidding me? If I'd heard … " She closed her mouth. Even if she had heard, she wouldn't have been able to afford the rent without draining the little bit of cash left in her savings.

He seemed to understand and didn't press. "I'd like to introduce you to the slob on my sofa." He took her by the crook of the arm and led her across the airy room.

Kimi, now in baggy sweats and wearing huge bags under her eyes, uncurled herself from the sofa and grinned. "Hello, Mrs. Prevost."

Colleen couldn't suppress her cringe, but Kimi apparently thought her reaction was funny and laughed. "Let me tell you, Colleen. If we had been home, people probably would have expected you to wave like the queen and give a coy grin."

Alan groaned.

"Don't groan," she said, stabbing her finger into her brother's chest. "You know it's true. The great benefactors, huh? They love the local people *so* much, huh?"

"You sound skeptical, Kimi. Do you not agree with the way your parents run their businesses?"

Kimi cocked up an eyebrow and twirled the end of one skinny braid around her index finger. "Do you agree with the way *your* parents run their business?"

"No. But, unlike yours, my family business is run into the ground. The only charity we're giving right now is to the local drunk, Marlon, by not calling the cops when he trespasses."

"I like your boots," Kimi said in a quick subject change that would have given a weaker woman whiplash.

Colleen stared down at the pair of the day: sea blue with little dinghies. Seemed appropriate given the state of her flooded house. "Thanks. I do the little doodles for the company I used to work for, and they give me free boots."

"I didn't know that," Alan said, and she jumped. She'd nearly forgotten the man was there, which was usually a difficult feat. Normally, his presence made her blind to her surroundings. He'd probably be a safety hazard should they ever try to cross a street together.

"What size do you wear?" Kimi asked.

"Nine."

"Dammit."

"Kimi," he growled. "I thought you were going to bed."

"I am," she said blithely, and gave her loose braid a defiant flip. "I wanted to meet your wife."

There was a bit of humor in the way Kimi said "wife" that made Colleen wary. What had he been saying about her? Did she know their marriage was bogus?

"Okay, well here she is. The former Colleen Sanders for your inspection."

"I like her. You should keep her. You'd make cute babies. I hate it when they're not cute. What are you supposed to say to that, Colleen? Are you supposed to tell the proud parents, 'Oh, your baby is so alert' or 'Look how fat he is!' or some crap like that? I hate lying. It's worst when they're like wrinkly, little aliens. Pitiful little things."

"Good *night*, Kimi," Alan said, tiredness in his voice.

The girl shrugged and backed toward the hallway. "Colleen, I wear a size seven shoe. Seven-and-a-half. Something like that."

Colleen laughed.

"Please ignore her," he said. "Regardless of her fine upbringing, she has little in regards to shame."

"I heard that," Kimi called out from down the hall, ostensibly a bedroom. "Don't forget you have that same upbringing, boor."

"Our parents really do love us very much," he said to Colleen, his voice deadpan.

"Is all of your family so interesting?" she asked.

"Yes, in good ways and a few bad ones I'm sure Kimi will take great delight in explicating. Hey, do you want something to eat? We had Indian food. Golden Palace makes a fabulous chicken tikka."

"I've had it, and I'd love some. Thanks."

She was actually starving, having not had a good meal at all since breakfast, and even that had been mostly coffee. She'd refused Mom's and Daddy's dinner invitation because she would have had to bring Alan. Alan could have probably held his own, but Colleen was growing weary of acting. This fake relationship seemed to take far more out of her than any of her exes ever had.

While Alan fiddled with the microwave, she sifted through the magazines and other assorted items accumulated atop his coffee table. In addition to the gearhead magazines she expected, and found, there were also some catalogs and sports magazines. She picked up one of the latter and flipped through it.

• • •

"Glad someone's reading those. I haven't had a chance to." He pulled a plate down from the cabinet and nodded toward the magazine in her hands.

"Then why do you subscribe?"

"Because I'm a sucker. Some girls selling magazines door to door told me they needed to sell three more to meet the marching band quota. They needed new mellophones or something."

"The solicitors don't bother me out at the farm. I think they're afraid of me. I know what they call me."

His hand, poised near the microwave handle, stilled. "What do they call you?"

She turned the page and grunted appreciatively at the centerfold picture of some nude rugby player. "Cold Colleen, among other things."

Well, he'd heard that one, and he didn't believe it one bit. There was a difference between being practical and being callous. If she were really as exacting as people thought, she would have fired what little staff she had left and saved on the payroll expenses instead of hoping, *waiting*, for things to turn around. She would have emptied out that shed and trashed the contents. "You don't seem too upset over it."

"It's not exactly a fresh wound."

The microwave beeped as the turntable stopped. Alan used that small distraction to gather his thoughts, smooth his words, before speaking. "How did it start? The reputation, I mean."

"It started long before I took the reins at Split Acres, if that's what you're asking." She nodded her thanks as he set the plate in front of her on the coffee table and extended a fork to her.

He sat in the club chair adjacent to the sofa and knit his fingers. "That is what I'm asking."

"I don't know when it all came to a head. I suppose it's something that built over time, so I can't really remember when the official title stuck. Certainly by the time I graduated from high school. Going away for college was great because I got to leave all that stuff behind. No one from Emerald Springs went to the same university I did, so I didn't have my new peers prejudging me over stuff that happened in the past. I had to think long and hard about coming back here. Why would I want to come home when I knew people thought so little of me?"

Maybe she didn't see things the way he did, given he was just an outsider looking in, but what he'd gleaned from people about Colleen was that she was frigid, yes, but a force to be reckoned with. That made men want to talk down to her to get her to back off, and women to not extend offers of friendship because Colleen didn't behave the way "proper" women did. They'd be guilty by association. Nothing he could say, though, would change his wife's perception of that. She was the one experiencing it, though he'd seen a small taste of it earlier at that zoning meeting.

She poked a particularly juicy piece of chicken with her fork and frowned at her plate. "Daddy made a mess and tried to sweep it under the rug. I studied the books before I took on the operations manager role and learned this place hadn't turned a profit since the year I left for college. I was ashamed because Daddy acted like nothing was wrong. You couldn't tell how rough everything was if you were looking on from a distance. He was still driving a nice car, never missed a fancy event in town. Found out Mom cashed in her retirement fund and used a small inheritance she'd been saving from my grandmother to keep the place flush. *Everyone* in their families who had means to do it poured money into the farm because Daddy had talked it up so much and it was supposed to be a big deal. Of course, Daddy never said anything to me and Jacob."

"Did your father catch up to you after the meeting?"

"Yes, he sure did."

"And, what happened?"

"There was some yelling."

"On whose part?"

"Mostly his. I tend to let him get it all out of his system without interrupting. He's healthier that way."

"Does he understand why we proposed the changes?"

"Sure, he understands why, but Daddy's always been resistant to change when it comes to the farm. That's why when he and Richard split, Richard's success blew Daddy out of the water. Richard was willing to take some calculated risks to ensure future success, but Daddy was more interested in maintaining the status quo because it had worked in the past. The problem with the status quo in farming is that eventually the farm gets tired."

"Were you very hands-on with Split Acres as a child?" He already knew, of course. Pixie had told him, but he wanted to hear it from Colleen's lips—learn of her passion directly from her without filtering.

She leaned back against the sofa. "I picked up tidbits here and there. I didn't do 4-H or anything like that because I was too busy with school and sports, but I did stuff at the fair and hung out at the farmer's market some Saturdays with Mom. I know the farm like the back of my hand. Spent a lot of time in the meadows with this big book of plants my grandmother sent me one birthday. That's why I know all the flowers around here and what grows well."

"And why so many of your boots have floral prints?"

That observation earned him a grin.

"Yeah. I guess I have an 'April showers bring May flowers' mentality."

"Is Split Acres in an April period?"

Drawing in a long breath, she rubbed her eyes. After she exhaled the spent air, she admitted, "Yeah, it's an April. It's been a long, wet April, and I'm starting to wonder if I should build an ark to wait out all the flooding, or if I should just climb into a rocket and bail out."

He could taste her resignation—the closeness to quitting. This was his chance to take it all, or at least what was Colleen's. With her off the job, Joe would have little choice but to throw in the towel because there'd be no qualified person left to run the farm.

But Kimi was right. He didn't want the farm if Colleen didn't come along with it.

Machines he understood. He could rewire a kitchen with his eyes closed and one hand tied behind his back. He was used to working solo, so this *partnering* scenario flummoxed him. Whose will should bend? Colleen's so he could break the farm and rebuild it from the ground up with the crops he knew best? Or his?

Colleen knew the farm in a way he probably never would, nor evidently even Joe.

She did have a lot at stake. Not just pride, but also payback because just like her, Colleen's mother had put everything she had into a failing venture to save it for a man she loved. Colleen apparently didn't want her mother to regret it.

And Alan didn't want Colleen to regret everything she'd invested, either.

Regrets were far harder to bury than blighted potatoes.

CHAPTER FOURTEEN

"How are things going, hon?" Kate kneaded Colleen's tired shoulders as she slumped over her desk, cheek flat against the desktop, moaning.

"I don't think it would be hyperbole if I said this has been the worst week on the farm in recent memory."

Her assistant kneaded some more. "Well, I hate to pile it on …"

Colleen groaned and sat up, craning her neck around to look at the older woman. "What now?"

"Three things. Kimi's here to take you to lunch."

"That's not bad, so I'm guessing the others are doozies."

"Well." Kate edged around to the front of the desk and pressed her palms onto the edge. "Second, Jacob's here. Said it's important he talks to you."

"About what?"

"Don't know."

"Sure." She closed her eyes and tipped her head over her seat back. "He didn't give a damn about the farm until I married Alan."

Alan, whose bed she'd been sleeping in for a week. Playing sleepover was fun, but there was a certain unnaturalness to their scenario. Maybe it felt a bit too normal, even with him crashing on the sofa every night. They had dinner together, with or without Kimi, all seven nights she'd been there, and Colleen couldn't remember feeling such ease in a long time. Alan and Kimi's relationship was profoundly different than the one she had with her younger brother. Although Alan and Kimi had an age gap almost twice that of Colleen and Jacob, their relationship seemed comfortable. Fine-tuned.

Jacob was the kid who came around and changed the household dynamics when Colleen was five. Sure, they got along okay, but they didn't really understand each other. Mom had always said Colleen was the sword and Jacob was the shield. She was aggressive; he was defensive. Made sense he became a cop.

"Oh, I just think he's trying to get a handle on the changes around here, especially with that big blowup you had with Adam yesterday."

Colleen groaned again. "I think I was justified."

"I happen to agree. I just regret there were so many witnesses."

At the time, Colleen hadn't known how else to respond beyond swearing loudly enough at the man that she could have been heard from Seattle. She'd come out of City Hall with the paperwork for the zoning change approvals tucked under her arm to find someone had put the final nail in her truck's coffin. That is to say, they poured cement in her engine. As she stood there with the tow truck guy, who'd insisted on taking a peek, Adam—who'd shown up to see the results of the zoning proposal—saw her and tried to have that impromptu meeting she'd been avoiding all week.

She had let him talk, saying nothing as she texted Alan: *Someone killed my truck. I'm at City Hall. Come get me?*

And then she walked around to her tailgate to grab a couple of grocery totes, only to find some joker had slapped an "I'm driving home to have some Emerald Tea" bumper sticker on her rusted chrome.

Adam, noticing the cause of her added frustration, said, "It's just a sticker, it'll come off with some elbow grease, I'm sure."

Colleen let him have it. Jacob had shown up five minutes later, just ahead of Alan, with the red and blue lights of his cruiser flashing.

Alan had deescalated the situation by telling Adam to call him directly at the farm, and she had dealt with Jacob. More or less.

Well, actually, she got into Alan's truck, wrenched her truck key off the ring, and tossed it at her little brother, saying, "As one of the taxpayers paying your salary, perhaps you can figure out who immobilized my sole vehicle."

Then she'd rolled up her window and let Alan drive her back to the farm.

She sighed at the memory.

"And who else is out there? Another Whitman?"

"Nope, but close. Marlon."

"What's he want?"

"Says he wants to fill out a job application."

"Are you kidding me?"

"Alas, no."

Colleen opened her eyes in time to see Kate slipping a cup of coffee under her nose. "Ugh, don't want it. Stomach has been in knots all day. I worry I've been indulging in too much chicken tikka. Kimi is addicted. We've had it three times in the past five days."

"You're probably just run down. What do you want to do about Marlon?"

The office door creaked inward, and Alan poked his head in.

She couldn't hold back the grin. The one little bright spot in her day was the man in the door, although she'd just seen him a few hours ago during the drive to work.

"I just came in to see where Kimi was taking you for lunch, but since I'm here, I'll deal with Marlon."

She stood. "Don't worry about it. You've got your hands full at my house and with the contractors going back and forth. He'll be in your hair all afternoon if you let him be."

He stopped her at the door and pressed his large hands onto her tense shoulders. "Hey, don't worry. Maybe I can show him just what kind of work will need to be done soon around here and that'll scare him off."

"He didn't used to be so flighty, that Marlon," Kate said. "He didn't get bad like that until his wife left. Used to be a good worker. Reliable. If he could get himself cleaned up, he'd make someone a good farm custodian."

"Maybe that *someone* has the last name 'Whitman,'" Colleen mumbled. She turned her gaze up to Alan. "But if you want to waste your energy, I'm not going to stop you."

He winked at her. "I'm good at this sort of thing. I used to have hopeless cases shadowing me on cruise ships all the time. A few quit."

Why that made her grin, she didn't know. Maybe there was some validity to her nickname after all.

"How's that new chair working out for you, Colleen?" he asked, lingering his hand over the doorknob and wearing a coy grin.

She rolled her eyes but couldn't stifle her smile. She ran her hands up and down the supple leather covering the chair arms. "I love this chair. Thank you."

He winked a second time, and pulled the door shut as he left.

Initially, she'd felt awkward about accepting the chair when Alan had rolled it into the office that past Monday, but once he'd pressed her into it and engaged the lumbar support, she'd let out one of those unmistakable telltale sighs that meant it was absolutely perfect, and anything she said beyond "thank you" would probably be a lie.

"Want to talk to Jacob in the office or what?" Kate asked.

"Eh." She stood, begrudgingly, and stretched her arms over her head. "Let's keep it casual. I'll walk and talk with him. Maybe the fresh air will do me some good given my sleep deficit."

Colleen saw Kimi lingering near the building's front door before she saw Jacob hovering near Kate's desk. To Kimi, she offered a shrug. To Jacob, she offered a cocked eyebrow. "Can whatever it is wait until after lunch, Jacob? And your hair's looking a bit short. Buzz cuts don't suit you."

Jacob, tall and solidly built at around six-one, fiddled with his deputy cap in his hands. "My usual barber was out of town. I went to that TrendyCutz place, and I guess the lady didn't understand what 'take a bit off the top and sides' meant."

Note to self. Have Alan avoid TrendyCutz.

"Ah. Jacob, have you met Kimi?"

"Not formally."

"Well, it's your lucky day. Kimi, this is my brother, Jacob. Jacob, this is Kimi Prevost—Alan's sister."

He extended a hand and shook Kimi's. "Nice to meet ya. To answer your other question, Colleen, no, I really can't wait. I need to get back on patrol in fifteen minutes. I know you're busy, but certainly you have fifteen minutes for your little brother."

Right. *Little* brother. He'd surpassed her in height around eighth grade, and she wasn't exactly a delicate flower at five-six.

"Fifteen minutes. You got it. Sorry, Kimi. I'll be right back," she said.

Kimi held up her hands. "Don't worry. Kate promised me some juicy gossip."

"About who? You've only been here a week. You couldn't possibly care about anything coming out of the Emerald Springs rumor mill."

Kimi quirked her lips up into that slight grin that should have conveyed innocence for any other person, but for Kimi worked in the exact opposite fashion.

"You're talking about me, you mean."

Her sister-in-law's smile broadened.

Colleen sighed and drew Jacob through the door.

They walked up the path in silence for a while, heading toward nothing in particular. When they'd reached the back edge of the flower field, a five-minute walk from the offices, Jacob asked, "So, how are things?"

She stopped just shy of a mud pocket in the road and moved aside for an incoming truck to pass them by. "That's a loaded question, Jacob. We haven't had a real conversation since Easter. To what do I owe the pleasure of your concern?"

"That's not fair, Coll." He sighed and raked his fingers through his nonexistent hair.

"It's true, Jacob. You live right there." She pointed toward the orchards to the east where his cottage was positioned. "Right there. And the only time I see you is when the folks are around or it's some holiday. And lately, at the scene of certain embarrassing interactions with the Whitmans."

"I work odd shifts, and I'm sorry. I know that's no excuse. I'm way out of the loop about everything. I should have known my sister was thinking about getting married."

She shifted her weight. Should she tell him? Jacob might understand. But maybe not. "It was a sudden thing."

"Yeah. I really don't know anything about him besides what some of the guys at the department told me. Chad told me Adam's a bit agitated. He didn't know Alan was a Prevost when he inquired over there. I bet he would have tried to keep him a little closer if he knew. Would have picked his brain."

"Too late."

"Yeah. Funny thing is, Dad has no idea who the Prevosts are. He is so out of the loop when it comes to tea, it's hilarious. I'd love to be in the room when it dawns on him that his son-in-law is related to Richard's biggest international competitor." Jacob's shoulders twitched and his eyes narrowed as he laughed. "He'll probably try to make it part of his next political campaign somehow."

Colleen laughed, too, not at Daddy's expense, but from relief. Her last few conversations with Jacob had been so damned strained that this lighter discourse was a welcome change.

"Anyway, Alan seems like a nice enough guy, and folks in town like him. He's probably saved a few lives."

"How so?"

"Used to hang out at the bar a lot on weeknights and would drive folks home if they'd had too much to drink. He'd do that two or three times a night then go back and finish his game of darts or whatever. How'd you guys meet?"

What lie had they decided on? Suddenly, she couldn't remember. "Why, are you looking to pick up a hot date?"

He chuckled. "No. Where would I find the time to take her anywhere with my schedule? I'd make the worst boyfriend ever. Just tell me, are you happy?"

Was she? She knew for sure she was tired, but underneath that there was a feeling of optimism. Although she was dreadfully busy, things were starting to look up. That was the closest thing to happy she'd been in a long while. "Yeah. I'm happy, Jacob."

"That's good to hear. Listen, I wanted to talk to you about my Split Acres shares. I—"

The radio on his collar crackled, and he stilled, listening to the indecipherable police chatter.

"Damn. I gotta run," and he did, literally, streaking up the gravel path toward the employee lot.

Colleen sighed. What was he going to say about his shares?

She was halfway back to the office when Jacob flew past her in his cruiser, shouting out his window, "I'll call you, okay?"

"Right," she yelled back with a wave over her shoulder.

Back at the office, she had barely opened her mouth to ask Kimi if she was ready to eat when Alan strode in and looped an arm around her waist, turning her.

Worry creased his features. "Have you seen Marlon?"

"Marlon? He was with you. I went for a walk with Jacob."

Alan looked from Kate to Kimi, both of whom shook their heads. "First he was there, helping me drop some wires in the main barn, and then I called out to him, and he was gone."

Kate drew in some air and shook her head. "God, that man gets more second chances than any one human being should, and he just keeps messing it up for himself. I'm tired of being his apologist."

"His lack of sobriety is not your fault, Kate," Colleen said.

"I know that, but if someone could get through to him … " She threw her hands up, shook her head, and gave her computer mouse an angry shake.

"I'll go see if I can track him down before he gets to his truck," Alan said, his hand already on the door handle.

Before he could pull it, however, the foreman appeared behind the glass, panic written on his face.

Alan pulled the door open. "What happened?"

The foreman flicked his wary gaze to Colleen then back to Alan, probably unsure to which of them he should direct his news.

"Spit it out," she said.

"Someone needs to call the police, or… I don't know who, but the outbuilding you just got zoning approval to rehab has just fallen in on itself."

She shook her head. "What are you talking about? That building is barely ten years old and structurally sound."

He nodded. "And that's why you need to call the police. I was out there with the contractor who was doing his drawing and measurements, and the only reason we got out of that building before the rafters fell was because that damn dog ran out of there like a bolt, and we walked outside to see what got into him."

"The rafters … *fell?*"

"I saw them fall in, Colleen. Weren't natural the way they caved in. All the load-bearing ones came down. Once the first one did, the rest splintered and dropped."

"Remember what I said two weeks ago, Colleen?" Alan said, holding the door open for the foreman to retreat through. His expression was dark, as if he were taking this slight personally. "All this shit happening isn't coincidence. Someone wants you to fail faster than they thought you were going to. Call the police, please. I'll go find Marlon if he's still around."

"You don't think Marlon—"

"I don't know, Colleen. Have a good lunch. Let me take care of this."

"I can't just—" Whatever objection she was going to speak was lost thanks to the closing door.

Kate and Kimi both stood agog—there would be no guidance from them.

But she was used to seeking her own council, and it was her outbuilding that'd been destroyed, not Alan's, regardless of what the paperwork said. This was her farm. If someone was going to raise hell and leave her to clean up the mess, she at least wanted to see it.

She pulled her phone out of the pocket of her rain jacket and dialed 911. As tersely as possible, she relayed the cause of concern to the dispatcher. After ending the call, she nodded to Kimi. "I'm sorry for skipping lunch."

"Take care of business, girlfriend. You are *so* not like my mother."

She didn't stick around to find out what that meant.

CHAPTER FIFTEEN

Colleen lay face down on the bed, her back rising and falling with her deep breaths as she finally had a moment to relax for the first time in a week. It'd been another grueling one, and that was just from Alan's perspective. He'd tried to mitigate some of the craziness at Split Acres, interceding where he could in regards to the outbuilding collapse and miscellaneous staff issues so Colleen could wrangle paperwork and deal with things on the business end. She'd been working late into the night, every night, so it was no surprise, really, she'd be damn near catatonic.

He took a few more steps into his bedroom and lingered near the bedside he hadn't approached in a week. Beyond fetching his clothes from the dresser, he hadn't spent any time in the room. That night eight days ago when he'd loosened her bed bolts, he'd thought he'd get her into his bed and share it, no questions asked.

But then she'd taken one step into his apartment and bonded with his little sister in about seven seconds flat, and that confidence vanished. The amount of respect he had for Colleen grew daily and he worried that perhaps he'd never live up to her expectations, whatever they were. He'd never seen a woman light up in such a way over something as trifling as a desk chair. If he were to actually give her the ring he had buried in his sock drawer, and upgrade that cheap gold band she wore begrudgingly, would she be just as ecstatic as she'd been about the rolling piece of furniture, or would she feel put upon? Confused?

Really, he didn't know how she felt about him beyond basic tolerance. As far as he could tell, she had never forgiven him for that night he told her he'd gone to Emerald Tea Farm first. He seemed to have pressed some button that he couldn't get to pop back out. Yet every time he touched her in some small way, her eyes went round, and that pale skin of hers flushed. She behaved as if she expected him *not* to touch her but didn't really mind if he did.

That was what he intended to test.

He sat on the edge of the bed and rested his hand on the small of her back.

She stirred, turning her face toward him.

"Hey, Colleen," he whispered.

"Is it time to get up already? God, I can't believe I fell asleep with my clothes on again."

"It's only eleven. You've been asleep an hour."

She closed her eyes and exhaled. "Oh."

He stood and eased around to the foot of the bed, carefully pulling down her socks and rolling them off her feet that dangled over the edge.

Her quiet giggle and curling toes as his fingers drew across her arches made him grin. "Ticklish?"

"A little."

"Does this tickle?" He lifted one foot, bending her leg at the knee for easier access, and kneaded her arch with his thumbs.

"No, that feels nice."

He repeated it on the other foot until she drew in a breath and opened her eyes.

"Sucking up to the boss? Not that I'm complaining."

"That was my plan. Is it working?"

"Don't know yet. Rub my shoulders, too, and I'll let you know."

"Okay." He climbed onto the bed and straddled her prone body, pressing his knees against her hips as he sat on her rear. He applied his fingertips to her shoulders and massaged out the kinks.

"So, what do you need to butter me up for? Certainly you're not asking for a raise since you more or less pay your own salary."

He chuckled and pressed his heels against her tense shoulder blades, grinding and kneading. "Maybe I just want an audience with the queen and I'm not beneath carnal favors."

"How carnal are we talking?"

"Hmm." He slipped his hands beneath the hem of her shirt and pressed his palms against the warm small of her back. When she didn't flinch or try to shake him off, he eased his hands further up her spine, kneading with his thumbs as he worked his way up to her bra strap. There he lingered a moment, and when she didn't react to his proximity, he slipped a finger beneath the catch and loosened it.

The one dark eye he could see fixed on him, but he didn't stop. He rolled her shirt up to her armpits, and said, quietly, "If you'd ease back a bit, I could take this off."

He waited for the snappy retort, but none came.

She eased her hands up near her face and pushed up onto all fours as he backed off of her. As she sat back onto her heels, he shucked her shirt over her head. Her bra, dangling by its straps, he eased down her arms, being careful not to graze her breasts as he claimed it.

"Seems like a lot of trouble to go through for a shoulder rub, Alan."

"Mmm hmm." He leaned into her and pressed his lips into the curve of her neck near her shoulder. "All that fabric gets in the way."

"It's nice that you're so thorough."

"That's me. Meticulous." He slipped his index finger into her bun and pried out the pins. He removed four before that cascade of dark hair fell onto her shoulders. Soft and silky, and smelling of the gardenias he'd noted the first day they'd met. He brushed the hair aside, over her right shoulder and put his lips back where they were, kissing downward and stealing a peek at the breasts his right hand mounded.

Before, he'd had to rely on touch and interpret shadows to appreciate her body, but in the dim light from the bedside table lamp, he could see she looked as beautiful as she felt. He let her breasts fall and trailed the fingers of his right hand down her taut belly to her waistband.

She gasped as he crooked a finger inside.

"Are you tired, sweetheart?"

"Aren't you?"

"Exhausted, but … I've wanted to touch you all week, and the week before. Ever since that first time. My hands are meant to be on you, I think."

"That must make swinging a hammer difficult."

"It does. I've been so preoccupied, I've done everything from dropping a tractor seat on my foot to nearly severing the satellite dish line with a spade."

"That's not good."

"You're a hazard to me. I can't get you out of my mind."

"I've been called a lot of things, but a hazard is a first."

Her belly contracted when his fingers eased beyond her waistband and past the elastic of her panties.

"They're all wrong. Every one of them. The things they call you."

When she turned her face to the left to catch him in her periphery, he leaned his head in and captured her lips.

There was no coffee taste this time, just the faint fruitiness of her lip balm, applied hours before.

He kissed her as if he were starved for her flesh, nipping at her lips with his teeth and encircling her tongue with his with such enthusiasm that she panted.

He turned her body around to face him and leaned her down onto the pillow, lying on top of her as soon as she was settled.

Wrapping her legs around his waist, she drew his torso tight against hers and arched her back as he ground his crotch at the apex of her thighs. "Take off your clothes," she whispered and dragged her fingertips down his back.

Somehow, he managed to keep the smile off his face as he eased up and heeded the woman's command. She'd always be the boss, even in the bedroom. Even when he took the lead, as he had the first time, he'd be more focused on her than himself. That seemed to be the natural order of things, and he didn't want to fight it.

He'd kneel at her feet and serve her in the way she deserved, if she wanted it. He made quick work of unbuttoning his shirt, shucking his jeans, and heeling off his socks. When he returned to her on the bed, she'd shimmied her pants past her hips, and he helped them the rest of the way, pausing only to dip his tongue into the perfect recess of her navel.

When her pants joined his clothes on the pile on the floor, he said, "You let me do all the work this time."

"Are you waiting for me to refuse?"

"I hope you don't." He eased her panties down, too, and held them in his hands a moment, studying the simple, pink bikini-cut garment.

"Marveling over my practicality? You're going to kill my mood, Alan."

"Not at all." He wadded them and let them fall to the floor as he eased to the nightstand. "Just thinking about how phenomenal you'd look in red lace."

"I think you may be the only man to ever express concern about the state of my underwear. Most men are only concerned with what's inside it."

"I like the packaging as much as the contents."

"I'll keep that in mind."

He slid the nightstand drawer open and freed a condom from the box. "Prepared this time. I apologize for being careless before. I hope you didn't think I'm usually so cavalier."

Something flitted across her face he couldn't quite read, but whatever it was, was gone in an instant. She nodded and dragged her tongue across her lips.

He sheathed himself and settled at the vee of her legs. He tapped his hips, and at that cue, she wrapped her legs around his waist.

"Consummating the marriage a couple of weeks late. I wonder if there's a record for this sort of thing."

"I don't know. I'm sure some cuckolded royal holds it." She drew him in closer with her tightening legs, and he entered her as his lips grazed hers.

Cuckolds. He didn't want to think about Colleen with any other man, not now, not ever again. They wouldn't appreciate what they had in her—this rare gem of a woman who, even through her fears, forged on. This woman who'd had numerous occasions to break down in the past week, but who'd instead coped the best way she could—by working harder. This ruthless woman who'd told her father in a particularly loud argument that she wouldn't let him die a failure when he'd balked about all the changes at the farm and threatened to veto them during the upcoming shareholders meeting. She didn't just dispense the bitter medicine, she took it, too. Every time one of the Whitmans visited or called with yet another thing, she maintained a stony expression, when Alan knew on the inside she was dying a little at being in their shadow.

She was a rare breed, and he'd be an idiot if he let her slip through his fingers for any reason. He wanted this ballsy, quietly ferocious woman at his side forever, but he couldn't be sure if she felt the same way.

"Alan!"

He pressed his lips over hers once more and stifled her moans as her body wrenched beneath his.

He loved that he could make her squirm—unhinge her—that he had some way to open her up, forcing her to reveal some side of her no one else could see.

"God."

When he rolled off of her, he stared at the ceiling, waiting for his vision to refocus before he turned to face her.

Her cheeks were flushed, pupils dilated, lips parted.

When he caught his breath, he said, "English."

"Hmm?"

"English. When I dream about you, I dream in English."

Her face burned a little redder, but by her smile, he could tell she'd taken his words as the compliment they were meant to be.

She was beautiful. What he'd done to get so lucky, he didn't know, but whatever magic he held over her, he hoped he could keep it up a little while longer.

CHAPTER SIXTEEN

Mondays always seemed like such inauspicious times to stage shareholder meetings, but Mondays were typically when her father was around to be present for them. Since there were a number of items requiring a vote, Colleen had to flag him when she could.

So they sat around the conference table at the operations building—Daddy, Colleen, and Alan with Kate taking notes—and did more arguing than conferencing.

"Daddy, you're being completely unreasonable," she said. She stood and paced near the window. "I've laid out a number of perfectly competent plans to revitalize this farm, and your only objection is 'that's not the way we do things.' You keep forgetting that it's my nose in the books, not yours. I know what's coming in and what's going out. At the current rate, we're not going to have a farm next year, and all the folks we currently employ will be out on their asses." Maybe she was exaggerating there somewhat. Alan could probably pump funds into the venture indefinitely, but she didn't want that. She wanted the farm to be solvent on its own, so when they parted ways, that money albatross wouldn't be hanging between the two of them.

"Colleen, what you're proposing is some experimental mumbo jumbo that hasn't been tested here, not even on a small scale, and you want to go full force—the entire farm—all at once. Now that's what I call risky."

"Then suggest something. Something other than planting garlic in the fall. Suggest something other than offering hay rides and setting up another damned pumpkin patch and corn maze. That stuff doesn't make us any money because the Whitmans do it bigger and better. We end up spending a boatload of cash every year for little return."

He bobbed his shoulders. "So we incorporate some of your ideas. But tell me, if we're bleeding money the way you say, where's the cash going to come from for improvements?" He had the audacity to look smug.

"Are you admitting now you've run the farm's credit into the ground? Mark that down, Kate, in case he forgets about it later."

"I did the best I could with what I had, Colleen."

"No, Daddy. You had opportunity after opportunity to turn the tide on this place. You had Mom's very wise counsel, but you didn't listen to her the same way you're not listening to me. You wanted to keep your feet anchored in a bygone era. And for what? So that you could retire and leave me and Jacob with all the debt?"

Now *that* got his attention. It was as if he hadn't considered that aspect before—that the farm's failure would be the legacy his children would have to clean up. And how long would it take them to dig out of it?

"So, what do you want me to do? Huh? Just vote yes even when my gut says no?"

"Your gut needs a recalibration, and I didn't want to have to drag Jacob into this, but he offered to sell me his shares in the farm and his cottage, too. He wants to move closer to town and having farm shares isn't doing anything for him. He's not getting any dividends out of this corporation, and all this mess does is complicates his tax filing every year."

"And your point?"

"Think about it, Daddy. He offered *me* his shares. Not you. If I buy him out, or if Alan does, we'll be able to outvote you every time. You didn't close your loopholes this time. My forty percent would become forty-five, and more if I buy out the nonvoting shareholders, most of whom have already agreed to the sale."

"I remember an era when children actually respected their parents."

"I've been nothing but respectful, not just to you, but to Granddad, Granny, and Mom's parents, too. I think about them every time I walk this farm because they struggled with their farms, too. I've been trying to run this place with as much dignity as I can manage in spite of what everyone thinks of me. In spite of all the obstacles. In spite of having little to no support from you."

"Now just a—"

"It's true," Alan said with a sigh. "Look, Mr. Sanders, Colleen didn't want me to speak, to tell you this, but I can afford to buy you out, lock, stock, and barrel, especially at the farm's current value. I can afford to buy out those investors you have hanging off the desiccated teat, and I heartily suggest you let me do that now before this place starts to turn a significant profit again. Colleen's plan is a good one."

Her heart fluttered. He'd never told her what he'd thought of her plan in all this time, and approval coming from him meant a lot.

"She could have this place making money—good money—within a couple of years. The risk is on us, not you."

"It's my farm. It's my name on it. I founded it."

Alan sighed. "I understand that, and your name will always be on the letterhead, but what I'm asking you to do is let Colleen and I buy you, Rebecca, and Jacob out the majority of your shares. We can work it out so you retain some major decision-making duties and would receive a nice check every quarter but would otherwise be uninvolved with the day-to-day operations."

Was he serious? Had he really put it out there just like that? She'd been dropping some not-so-oblique hints that she wanted to push her father into retirement, but Alan had gone straight for the jugular, no holds barred. How much would that cost her in the long run? She'd be forever in his debt, given all the zeroes in that amount she owed.

"You want me to get Rebecca and Jacob on conference call?" Kate asked.

Everyone looked to Daddy. He swiveled in his seat, not responding for a while.

"This is money for you to retire with," Colleen said in a soft voice. "This is money for Mom to finally take that vacation she always wanted. For you both to be comfortable."

"I hear what you're saying, and while my brain thinks it all sounds rational and that I should do it, my heart says you're trying edge me out of my own company."

Time for the truth?

Colleen counted to three, tempering her words, and said, "Yes, Daddy. I think it's time you moved on. I can't say it more plainly."

"You used to be a daddy's girl. What happened?"

"This isn't personal. Put yourself in someone else's shoes and imagine you're on the outside looking in. Do you think anyone out there," she swept her hand toward the greater farm beyond the walls and to Emerald Springs itself, "really cares who makes the decisions here? Everyone knows this is your farm, just like they know that Adam may be stepping up to the plate for the Whitmans, but his father built the stadium. The only time folks'll care who's doing what is when someone *fails*, and Daddy? I don't plan on failing. I refuse to accept that as an option anymore."

He raked a hand through his hair and blew out a breath through his mouth. "So, talk me through this. You're offering to buy me out and in exchange, what power do I keep?"

Alan set his elbows onto the table. "Well ... "

Colleen tuned him out and pushed back from the table, swallowing hard.

They didn't seem to pay any notice to her walking out of the conference room. She stepped over the dog, strode into her office, and locked herself into her powder room.

When she was done retching, had wiped her face and rinsed her mouth, she opened the door.

Kate stood there with her hands jammed into her jeans pockets. "What?"

"Don't tell me it's the chicken tikka, Colleen."

"Shouldn't you be taking notes?"

"What would they say? 'Pissing match ensued'? By the time I go back in there, they'll still be going at it. I'm not missing anything."

Colleen swallowed and dragged her shirtsleeve across her forehead. "It's not the chicken tikka."

"You look like garbage."

"Good. So, I look how I feel. No need to pretend to be cheery."

"Does he know?"

"No."

"How long have *you* known?"

Colleen tried doing the calendar math, but gave up. She was too tired. "Dunno, what's today? Monday? Missed my period, which almost always wallops me at dinnertime on day twenty-six. Figured it was just the stress and that it'd start eventually. A few days later, I had a cup of coffee that tasted faintly of dirty pennies, and thought, 'hey, that can't be right,' and so I peed on a little plastic stick. And then another."

"I didn't realize you two were married in the Biblical sense." Kate's lips twitched at the edges.

She could hardly dare to get angry. She just slumped and rubbed her eyes. "Well, you've looked at him. I'm frequently in awe that he's my husband, and then I remember, oh yes—I married him for his fat wallet. But, when I'm on my hands and knees with my head held over the toilet, I almost forget why I wanted to save this dump in the first place."

"So, now what?"

"Don't know. I don't want him to feel like I trapped him."

"Takes two to tango, Colleen, and seeing the way that man looks at you, I'm pretty sure if he sticks around, it's not because of what you're growing."

"You really think that?" She wanted him to stay, but not because of *that*.

"I'd be willing to bet on it."

• • •

If Alan had known dangling a carrot in front of Joe's nose would have worked, he would have tried it much sooner. The two men had been in a stalemate for several minutes, arguing back and forth in Colleen's absence, but then he had a thought. Leaning across the table, he'd whispered, "You do know who my family is, right?"

And Joe had given him that same blank look Colleen had when she'd studied his work authorization documents.

Obviously, the Prevost name didn't mean much to people who didn't farm tea. Sure, they may have *known* who the Prevosts were, but they wouldn't immediately associate Alan as being connected to them.

And then it dawned on Joe.

He shaped his lips in an "O" and leaned back in his chair. "What's your endgame?" Joe asked.

"Stability." There. Alan had answered as honestly as he could. The time in his life for roaming had passed. Now was the time to put down roots, and he liked where he was. He could make a life for himself in the valley—make some friends, start a family.

There was just that small matter of getting Colleen on board.

So, if they could get the paperwork shaken out, the two of them would own the farm, while Joe kept his president title. An unusual arrangement, probably, but people had no idea just how atypical their situation was.

Joe stood to leave as Kate returned to the room, *sans* Colleen.

"What'd I miss?" the secretary asked, pushing her reading glasses back onto her nose.

"Alan has bought the farm," Joe said. "Literally." He laughed and shook his head. "The Whitmans have been in a tizzy for weeks, trying to figure out what's going on over here. Now they'll really be wondering what I have up my sleeves."

"God, Joe," Kate sighed. "Don't go blabbing the news all over. Let some things unfold in their own time, huh? Next thing you know, this place will be swarming with reporters and we won't be able to get anything done."

Ha. Reporters. The last thing Alan wanted was Colleen in the newspaper again. That tiny little column she wrote brought down the wrath of hell on him from his parents, who apparently weren't beneath Googling his new wife's name.

His father had yelled across the Atlantic with help of his cell phone for a good ten minutes before Alan could get a word in edgewise. "Can we discuss this rationally?" he had asked in Afrikaans. His father had been so angry, he hadn't bothered with English. "Are you more pissed I skirted around the trust fund restrictions, or that I played your game better than you and won?"

That had started his father on another long tirade that ended with his mom taking the phone and saying into it with a forced calmness, "So, when do we get to meet your wife?"

"That's up to Colleen," he'd said.

"And I know you know, Alan. Where is my daughter?"

That had given him pause. Kimi said she'd left a note. Just what had that note said?

He'd eyed Kimi on his sofa, and her eyes went round with knowing. She always knew when she was being talked about.

Alan had hedged. "I'm not certain what you mean."

"Kimi. Where is Kimi? She left almost two weeks ago without a goodbye."

"Really? She didn't leave a note?"

His mother had gone quiet for a moment, then spat, "Her note said she was leaving and not to worry about her."

"So maybe you should try that. She's a twenty-five-year-old woman, Mother. She can take care of herself."

"She's never been anywhere!"

"And whose fault is that? Don't you see now that trying to control your children's innate proclivities to roam has the potential to backfire? If you're lucky, she'll sow her oats and go home. Force her back, and she'll never forgive you. Can't you loosen her leash? Cut her some slack? Do you really want her to be that sort of married woman who's never gone anywhere, seen anything?"

Silence again.

"Your father cancelled her credit cards. She'll have no choice but to come home; that's why I wondered if she'd been in contact with you."

"I see. I'll let you know if I hear anything."

And that was the last lie he'd tell. He was through with lying. Tired of it. It all weighed heavily on him, had been affecting his sleep. Making him paranoid. If he didn't lay it all out for Colleen soon, he'd probably make himself sick from holding it in.

Joe's voice brought Alan back to the present. "I'll keep quiet about it for however long you need, but you gotta admit, this is pretty good timing. People will just think I phased out of active involvement on the farm so I could concentrate on legislature stuff. Hey, I wonder if we can get our ducks in a row in time enough to have a more visible presence at the county fair this year." He rubbed the stubble on his chin and squinted at the ceiling. "Haven't done much in the past couple of years, but maybe this would be a good chance to show off the new value-added products, if you can get some samples together by then." He looked to Alan for a response.

"I'm certain Colleen can come up with something."

"Yeah ... " Joe pulled the door open and rubbed the sheltie's head when Arfer pushed his snout against his long-absent owner's leg. "Colleen's usually good for that."

When Joe left, Alan tamped the scattered papers on the table into a pile and raised his gaze to Kate. "Where's my lady? I thought she must have stepped out to take a call or something."

Kate folded her glasses and tucked them into the pocket of her denim shirt. "She had some bad chicken tikka."

CHAPTER SEVENTEEN

"Colleen, are you alright, sweetheart? Kate said you had a bad dinner."

God, every time that man called her "sweetheart," her gut did funny things. She wanted to believe he meant it—that it wasn't just some throwaway term of endearment he used on any person with the right genitalia. In the past, she would have balked at being called such a thing by any man beyond her father, but maybe there was something special about being called *sweetheart* by the right man. The kind of man who just did it for her.

Colleen lifted her cheek from the cool, wood desktop and set her gaze on the man in the club chair in front of her. The two club chairs were new. They were delivered the day after Alan had rolled in her new desk chair and were upholstered in sky blue fabric and decorated with tiny white peonies.

She hadn't known how to respond to the office addition, but Alan had said, "They're comfortable. If you're going to keep beckoning me to your office, I want to at least have a chair with a bottom that isn't going to fall out. We'll get you some carpet that matches soon."

She'd need that carpet. Couldn't have a baby crawling around on a particleboard subfloor.

She swallowed. "I'm fine. Just a little woozy." Vast understatement, and she knew it. Her head throbbed. Was all that light really necessary? She wondered if the sun had come out that day just to spite her. She couldn't remember when she'd last had a migraine, but it had to have been sometime during puberty when her hormones were churned up in a biological tsunami.

"Want me to get you some Alka-Seltzer or something?"

Did Alka-Seltzer have aspirin? She couldn't have aspirin, could she?

"Thanks, but I'll be okay. I may try to squeeze in a doctor's appointment later if it doesn't let up."

Her doctor had told her to come in immediately for blood work, but Colleen kept putting it off. She could have walked in whenever she wanted, but she worried that having someone official—*qualified*—acknowledge her pregnancy meant she would actually start planning for it. Did she even have maternity coverage on her insurance?

"Colleen?"

She looked up and met Alan's concerned blue gaze. "I'm sorry, were you saying something?"

"Why don't you go home? I mean, to my place. How many days have you taken off this year, huh? Just the one day I was hired? I don't think anything is going to fall apart in your short absence."

That was left to be seen. She drew the little cup of lemonade Kate had brought in earlier across her desktop and put it to her lips. Normally, she would have given the man an outright *no*, but she felt awful enough that she knew she'd only be making herself a martyr. How could one tiny little bundle of cells raise so much hell? And in such a short time? Kate said Colleen was one of the "lucky" ones.

If this is what sex did, she didn't want it ever again.

"Colleen?"

God, that voice sent tingles down her spine and made her skin ache to be touched. No, no. She couldn't give up the sex. She liked the sex too much, but certainly, the pregnancy part sucked a lot. And it'd probably get worse, according to Kate.

She put her head on the desktop again. "I'll be okay. I probably will head out a little early today. Did you need anything?"

"Your father was wondering if you had any ideas for the fair exposition. I told him you'd take care of it."

She felt his fingers at the base of her skull, rubbing her neck.

She let out a little moan. "That feels good."

Then she realized what he said and picked up her head. "Daddy hasn't wanted to do anything for the fair before now because they always put our stall near the Whitmans. What'd you do to him?"

Alan laughed, and those wrinkles at the corners of his eyes deepened.

She'd never get used to the idea that this man found her amusing.

"Nothing. This was all his idea, believe it or not. I think the prospect of change is growing on him, slowly but surely. He's a man with a lot of fears, and that's healthy."

"You're right. I'd rather him be afraid of something but still want to try instead of letting us become stagnant and left behind when there's so much potential here. If I had known all I needed to get him to consider it was to bring in an outsider, I would have married some random guy a year ago when my savings were still intact."

His grin waned somewhat, but he laughed again and raked a hand through his thick hair. "Just something for you to be thinking about amidst all the other things."

"Like finding some place to live?"

He opened his mouth, closed it, and pushed to standing. "Tell me where you want to live, and I'll make it happen."

She swallowed. The ideal should have been the three of them—him, her, and the baby—under the same roof, but she wouldn't dare wish for such a thing. Alan had made absolutely no overtures about their long-term plans beyond those concerning the farm, and she wasn't brazen enough to escalate their relationship to that level herself.

Odd. She could compartmentalize and push aside that timid part of her that feared failure enough to stand in front of zoning boards and demand things for the business, but when she wanted something for herself that was *personal*, she didn't know how to approach that territory. In the past, she'd never worried about a man telling her *no* and that was because she didn't really care if they did. This one, though ...

She cared.

She picked up her cell phone and fiddled with it, clearing the screen of messages she'd missed.

There was one from Alan she hadn't heard, and someone had programmed his picture into his contact card along with a variety of other biographical information. Middle name. Birthdate. Email address.

Must have been Kimi. Colleen smiled at her sister-in-law's interference.

She rolled her eyes up to him, and his expression was expectant. "Don't worry about it. I owe you too much already. I'll figure something out. Maybe I'll move into Jacob's cottage. That one doesn't evoke nearly as much guilt for me. It was already empty when we bought the place. Might even be comfortable there. And the wiring's newer." She added that last bit for Alan's benefit, lest he concern himself.

He shifted his weight. "You can ask me for anything."

She swallowed. *Almost* anything. "I'll keep that in mind."

"Right. I've got to go meet with the architect about that new processing building. I figured you'd want to tag along."

Normally, she would have, but at the moment, she couldn't muster up the enthusiasm, and besides, Alan had proven himself capable. She needed to get better at delegating, so this seemed like a good enough place to start. "No. I'm going to make a couple of calls and then do what you suggested. Go to your place and get some sleep." More likely, she'd just press her cheek against the cool tile of his master bathroom until she heard the front door open, then she'd scramble to her feet and pretend to be well on her way toward recovery.

"All right."

He seemed to be lingering for some reason, so Colleen raised her eyebrows. "What?"

"Nothing," he said, shaking his head. "I'll call you later. See if you're up for some dinner. Not chicken tikka."

Ugh, food. "Okay," she said.

After another long pause, and a little wave, he backed into the hallway and pulled the door closed.

She sighed, picked up her desk phone, and grabbed an outside line. Greg picked up on the first ring.

"I've got your number memorized now, Colleen. Please tell me you're coming back and that I won't have to continue to wrangle these couthless savages on my own."

She laughed, and immediately regretted it when a new thrum of pain assaulted the space behind her eyes. She closed them and sighed. "No, Greg, unfortunately, I'm calling to ask for another favor."

"Gosh, Colleen, you could at least pretend to like a guy. What can I do for ya?"

"More like what can we do for each other. I need some boots."

"Which, what size, and how many?"

"Just like that?"

"It's a small favor. Ask me for something big, and I'll probably deliver on that, too."

She waited for his laughter, and when it didn't come, she scrunched her brow. Greg seemed particularly sullen for some reason. It wasn't like him. "I'll let you know particulars," she said when he didn't follow up. "I just found out I have to put together a fair stand for Split Acres, and I think it'd be a great idea to showcase some of the items that'll be available in the farm store next spring. If you think we could swing it, I'd like us to be an authorized retailer for the brand. Just the boots and rain hats, though. They'd tie in wonderfully with the changes we've got planned."

"Sounds like things are looking up."

"Yeah," she admitted. "Things are definitely looking up. And I may have another retailer lead for you. Another company we're partnering with starting next year."

"Colleen, you work harder than anyone I know. We'll make it happen. Oh, by the way. We've got some ugly streaking in a few of the catalog shots, and we'll be out at the resort in the morning doing reshoots. The new boot proofs came in, and we approved them. I'll bring you the nines."

"Hey, can you bring me the sevens instead?"

"Been foot binding? You've never been vain before, Colleen. All that country air is getting to your head."

"No, ass," she laughed. "Someone admired my boots and I want her to have them."

"In that case I'll bring you the sevens *and* the nines."

"Thank you. I can always count on you being in my corner, Greg. You don't know how much that means to me."

"More people should be in your corner, Colleen. They're idiots if they're not."

• • •

"Alan?"

"Is that you, Kimi?" Alan cranked up the volume on his phone and pressed the speaker closer to his ear canal. "I can hardly hear you through the static. Where are you?"

"I'm at the sheriff's de—"

She got cut off.

"Dammit!" He pulled his truck over to the shoulder, recalled the last incoming number, and told his phone to dial it.

It rang and rang on the other end, only to have an automated voice to come on the line to say, "The number you have dialed does not accept incoming calls. Please check your number and try again."

He growled, copied the number into his phone's web browser, and did a reverse look-up.

"Em Spr Muni Compx" the site said, so he turned his truck around and headed back toward town.

He'd been on his way to Split Acres after dealing with some banking stuff in town—he'd finally established a local account—when the call had come through. He wanted to tell Colleen his landlord had a similar apartment with a third bedroom and see what she'd say. They'd been sharing a bed for the past few nights, and he'd all but given up on work at her little house, given her feelings about the place. The foreman had expressed some interest in moving closer, so maybe one day they'd renovate the onsite lodging for staff, but it wasn't an immediate concern at the moment.

She didn't seem to mind so much that he slung his arm and leg over her every night, or that they both woke up sweaty because she burned hot in her sleep. Beyond that, he couldn't say one way or another what she felt. What she wanted. Maybe she was just as skin-starved as he, and he was just the body who happened to be in the right place at the right time. He was tired of guessing, though. He'd never beat around the bush so much in his life, so maybe he should come right out and ask.

He pulled into the municipal complex—the cluster of buildings that contained City Hall, the local sheriff's department, and various other city offices—and had his truck door open before he'd even killed the engine.

Running inside the sheriff's office, he was immediately drawn into a cacophony of commotion. People yelling loud and swearing, police trying to calm them—a mass of bodies, seeking answers.

He edged closer to the officer at the reception desk and shouted over the din, "I'm looking for Kimi Prevost. She called me."

The officer raised one blond eyebrow and mumbled, "I bet she did."

"What's going on?"

A man eased between Alan and the woman beside him—one of the Whitmans, though Alan couldn't remember which—and shouted, "Problem at Emerald Eats. Your sister was at the wrong place at the right time." The man grimaced and recanted, "Or right place at the wrong time. I can never get that straight."

"Who are you?" he asked.

"Chad Whitman. I manage the place. You want to go outside where it's a little quieter?"

"I need to—"

Chad put his hands up. "Dude, you're not going to get close until some of this crowd clears out. Too many damn people in here."

Alan eyed the officer, who merely shrugged, and then he followed Chad outside to the stairs.

Chad extended a hand to shake. He took it.

"Alan Prevost."

"Yeah, I and most everyone else in town knows who you are. You married everyone's favorite nutcracker."

What was with people and their little slights toward Colleen? Alan opened his mouth to defend his wife, but Chad thumped his back, distracting him.

"I mean it in the fondest way possible. Colleen's a tough cookie, but she's always been kind to me, even after she and Adam had it out." He snorted.

"What do you mean?"

"Aw, kid stuff. Nothing to worry about. Before the farms split off, we kids used to play together. She and Adam were in the same kindergarten class, first grade class and so on. Rode the bus together, took care of each other. And then … "

"Okay. Yeah. People grow up. Grow apart."

"Well, yeah, but more so, little boys become brats, and little girls have to become bitchy to put the little boys in their place." Chad's shoulders shook in a way that forecasted laughter would be coming soon. "She's never been submissive that way."

Must have been some interesting stories in Colleen's past he would love to hear about, but it didn't seem like the right time.

"What happened? Why is my sister here?"

"Like I said, she was just swept up in the chaos. There was a fight at the restaurant I manage, and it got ugly. We don't know who started it and for what, but one moment there was quiet, and the next, Marlon Miller was in there throwing punches at one of my waiters. The waiter is a pretty chill guy, but you swing at him, he'll swing back. One of the ladies in the restaurant started yelling that Marlon's always getting picked on, and then another lady shouted that Marlon once ran over her parked bicycle and to shut her trap. It turned into a big mess. Kimi was at the counter having lunch, and the cook pulled her out of the scuffle. She just sat there, frozen, like she'd gone into shock. My Uncle Sam was there, and he hit the fire sprinklers. That broke up the worst of it. By the time the deputies arrived, the place was trashed."

He was glad to hear Marlon had finally turned up, but … "Was she hurt, Kimi?"

"No, no. I don't think so. She was just at ground zero. This should make fabulous press for us." He crooked his thumb toward the station. "My brother Daniel is inside having a cow, so that's why I'm out here. They're better at handling these sorts of problems, he and Adam." The pleasant smile he wore wilted a bit at the corners. He rocked back onto his heels and stared at the stream of bodies exiting the department. "Just what we need. Bad press right before the resort was due to run a major promotion in the travel magazines. Somehow, this'll be my fault."

Yeah, bad press. Exactly what his Googling parents needed to figure out precisely where their roaming daughter was.

"Dammit. Thank you, Chad, for the information. I have to get my sister. This is going to be a huge problem for us."

Chad's brow furrowed. "What, passport stuff?"

Alan just nodded. Close enough.

CHAPTER EIGHTEEN

Colleen knelt on the polished cement floor in front of Kate's desk and examined the new rubber boots Greg had hand delivered, though several days later than expected. There'd been some sort of commotion within the Emerald Tea businesses, and they had to delay the catalog shots. That same commotion had Alan operating in extreme stealth mode over the past week. Kimi's bags were missing from the apartment, and he had been extremely evasive about where she'd gone. "Best you not know," he'd said.

Colleen had pushed, because anyone with a heart would worry about someone as sweet as Kimi, but Alan's strained expression had indicated something convoluted was in play. She'd let the subject drop, only because he'd given her shoulder a squeeze and said, "She's fine. I promise, sweetheart."

And she believed him.

Greg sat in one of the comfortable new chairs in front of Kate's desk and watched Colleen with a big grin on his face. "Huh? What do you think?"

"You know, I worried about those color combinations, but these—they look great. I'm relieved."

"They do look great," Kate agreed.

"I'm glad I didn't know you were panicked, or you would have had me in a tizzy, too. Last thing I need at my age is to be in a constant state of tizzy-ness," Greg said.

Colleen rolled her eyes. "Your knack for the dramatic is legendary. You're forty-two."

Kate scoffed. "A baby."

He shrugged. "Feeling my age today."

"And yet you're always so spry when you're around me. Such a fraud." Colleen pulled herself to her feet with the aid of Kate's desk edge and returned his grin.

"Well, what can I say? You have a knack for making a man want to be more than he is."

"What are you talking about?"

Kate fed some papers through the shredder, and when the whirring died down, she said, "You sure are dense, Colleen. The man has been making passes at you for half an hour."

"What?"

Colleen rolled her tense shoulders back and fidgeted the ends of her loose hair. She'd loosened her bun so as to lie flat on the gurney in the doctor's office and never got around to putting it back up.

Greg took a few steps forward with eyes narrowed at her. He took her left hand in his and peered down at it. "When'd you get that?"

Oh. The ring.

She drew her hand back and stuffed it into her jeans pocket. "Few weeks ago."

"You got married? I didn't know you'd even gotten engaged. You didn't say anything."

She opened her mouth to explain it all away—to apologize—but then closed her lips when Kate passed behind Greg, shaking her head.

"I did. I married … a farmer."

"Well, who is this guy? Is he treating you well? I wish you'd said something." He swallowed, and the blood that had flooded his cheeks gave way to an equally telling pallor. "You should have said something. The folks at Markson, we would have gotten you a wedding gift."

She looked down at her feet. She'd worn flats because of her doctor's appointment, and missed having that extra space to curl her toes. That's what she did when she needed to think. Tried to wriggle each toe, one at a time, and meditate on her problems. Usually she came up with an answer. It wasn't always a good one, but at least someplace to start. "Yes," she said finally. "He's treating me well."

"Well, I hope so, Colleen, because you deserve it. You love him, huh? Bashful isn't one of your usual temperatures."

Love? That was a word she hadn't bandied about except in a familial context lately. She hadn't given much thought to feelings with everything going on. There was the baby wreaking havoc on all of her major body systems, they had no answers to the sabotage efforts that'd occurred on the farm, and then there was the legal drudgery they were working through trying to shake out the farm ownership issues.

What she did know was that whenever she was in a room with Alan, for the first few moments the air seemed too thin to breathe. Whenever he smiled in that way that made the corners of his eyes crinkle, her cheeks warmed. When he put his hand at the small of her back, her gut clenched.

She felt like some schoolgirl with a crush, until she remembered she was *married* to this man, and whenever she wanted, she could take him home with her and he'd kiss her silly and drape that gorgeous body of his over hers.

Beyond that, there was the way he anticipated her needs and met them before she could ask. And it wasn't just silly things like desk chairs but also more thoughtful acts like tracking down the old farm owners and shipping their precious photos to them. The woman who'd live there had called, crying, and Colleen had hardly been able to make out what she wanted. She just kept saying "Thank you, thank you" again and again, and wishing them all good fortune.

So, when she looked up at Greg, whose face was laced with worry, she admitted, "Yes, I love him. I love my husband."

He nodded and folded that left hand of hers between his two. "He's a lucky man. You let me know if he ever fouls it up, and I'll teach him the error of his ways."

She nodded, too. "I will."

As Greg pulled away, pushing his glasses up his nose, the door opened and Alan strode in.

He eyed them both, and Kate, before sighing. He handed the newspaper pressed beneath his arm to Colleen, and said, "Sweetheart, can I talk to you outside for a moment?" She cast her gaze down to the headline of the *Emerald Springs Chronicle*. It was from more than a week ago, and she'd already seen it—the one with a tearful Kimi on the cover and the headline "Tea Princess Laments Big Mess."

Had something more happened to Kimi?

"Um." She looked to Greg then to Alan, who shifted his weight from foot to foot with an unusual agitation, and decided she should probably introduce these two important men in her life. "Uh, Alan Prevost, please say hello to my old boss, Greg Quinton."

Greg hesitated before extending his hand to Alan. "Old boss. That's me."

Alan shook his hand, but there was no amusement to be found in his features. "I'm her husband."

"We were just discussing you."

"Were you?"

"Yes. Whatever voodoo you did to conjure up a woman like this ... powerful stuff, man. Whatever the trick is, I'd like to learn it."

"When I figure it out, I'll be sure to let you know." Alan tipped his head toward the door. "Sweetheart?"

"Right." She eased around the scattered boxes of boots, thinking of how she'd have to store Kimi's until her sister-in-law turned up again, and put her hand in Alan's when he reached for it.

He drew her through the door, and she whispered, "What's going on?" as he led her around the corner.

"I would have preferred for this to happen under more controlled circumstances."

"Preferred for what to happen?"

Shit. What now?

And they stopped. At the shaded picnic table Alan had recently installed for the staff, a tall, dark-haired man stood with his back turned to the building and a finely dressed blonde perched elegantly at the edge of the left bench. Colleen half expected the woman to have lacy white gloves clamped beneath her hands, she was so regal.

"Alan, what's going on? Who are they?"

This time, he answered. "My parents, Colleen. They came looking for Kimi, and couldn't find her, so they decided to come look for you, too."

"Your—your parents?"

The same people of whom the mere mention could make Kimi blanch and sway? The same people Alan always spoke of with a sigh?

The man turned, finally, and studied them. He was Alan, maybe twenty-five years older and with a far less sunny disposition.

Colleen had never been the sort of woman who'd let a surly man make her cower, at least not visibly, so she straightened her spine and raised her chin. "Hello," she said to them both.

The woman said something in what she thought was French and Alan growled, "English, mother. And don't be so catty."

"Would you like me to repeat myself, Colleen?" Mrs. Prevost asked.

"No," Alan intercepted before she could get "Yes" off her lips. She *wanted* to know what this woman had to say—what she thought of her daughter-in-law, at least for the moment.

Colleen pulled at Alan's shirtsleeve, and said, "I'd like to know what she said."

"I'll paraphrase," Mr. Prevost said, taking a few steps closer to his son. "My wife said she's uncertain which thing Alan wanted to acquire more, you or your farm."

Acquire?

She felt her face slacken with confusion and she turned to Alan, whose jaw had tensed. He narrowed cold eyes at his father.

"What are you talking about? Alan, what's he talking about?"

"Colleen, do you think we're stupid? We know what your farm was worth before Alan shored it up for you. We offered him the money to buy it for us."

She turned to Alan, and watched his chest expand as he drew in air.

"Colleen, listen—"

"You came here wanting to take my farm from me? You were the one who warned me they were waiting to scoop it up. You said you'd help so they couldn't get it. Is that just how you intended to get my guard down?"

She pulled away from him and backed up a few paces.

"Please listen, Colleen. We need to talk."

She shook her head. "No. No way. You've had weeks to make up a good lie, and I don't want to hear it."

"Colleen! There you are." Daddy rounded the corner, a big, sappy grin on his face.

When had he come into town?

He barely acknowledged the strangers on the cement pad and walked straight toward her. "Colleen, why didn't you tell us? Your mother is already in a frenzy, knitting tiny pastel things in case it's true."

"What are you talking about?" She thought she already knew. After all, this was Emerald Springs. God forbid she have a secret.

"Zoe Miller saw you coming out of the OB's office this morning. She wanted to know if congratulations were due."

Yep. That was it. The world seemed to stop spinning right then, and she wanted off the ride. All she could do was stare at the whiskers on her father's chin and watch his lips move.

Back in Seattle, she'd had privacy when she wanted it and friends when she needed them. Returning to Split Acres had brought her nothing but stress. She'd been unable to have anything for herself in more than two years, and if that wasn't masochism, she didn't know what was.

"Colleen?"

She tuned back in at the sound of her father's voice, and narrowed her eyes at him.

Somewhere in the background, vaguely, she heard Mrs. Prevost ask, "OB? What is that short for?"

Alan didn't respond. When Colleen flicked her gaze to him, his expression was a stunned mask—blue eyes wide and lips parted.

"Looks like we all have our secrets, huh, Alan?" She turned on her heel and took off toward the flower field.

Where else could she go? She was stranded on her own farm with no truck as Kate had driven her to work, and she didn't even have a functional house to go to anymore.

Stomping through the daylilies, she wrenched off her ring and hurled it into the orange expanse. "We'll see what good that does for the dirt."

CHAPTER NINETEEN

Colleen curled into a ball on Pixie's sofa and let the woman rub her hair. No one knew she was here. The first place they would have looked was at Kate's, so Colleen didn't bother begging for her hospitality. Pixie had taken one look at her, let her in, and didn't ask questions.

She fed her when she needed it, turned off the television when her eyes closed, and didn't pry too much when she wiped away tears that fell for seemingly no reason. Colleen hadn't been to work in days, and for all she knew, the place was falling apart without her.

She only half cared, especially after spending a couple of days in the hospital hooked up to IV bags because she couldn't keep anything down. Kate had been right. It had gotten worse, but no way could she have predicted it'd be *that* bad.

Alan had found out too late she'd been admitted, and called her phone again and again, pleading with her to answer. To *talk*. She got tired of seeing that picture popping up on her phone screen, and so she deleted it.

His parents had gone home, he said. He wished she'd listen, he said. He didn't mean to hurt her, he said.

Bullshit. That had been his plan all along, and now between very long naps, all she could do was brainstorm ways to make him go away. The mental gymnastics she did to figure out how much money she owed him and how long it'd take her to pay him back made her temples throb.

The little house's front door clicked open, and Colleen cast her tired eyes up to see Kate slipping in with a paper bag in her arm.

"Brought her some more saltines, if she can keep 'em down."

"Oh, she had some toast this morning. That's progress," Pixie said.

"Stop talking about me as if I weren't here," Colleen murmured.

"Sorry, honey. We'd very nearly forgotten you could talk. Haven't heard your dulcet tones in a while." Pixie patted her head, and she sat up so the woman could stand.

"Any news about Kimi?" Colleen asked after clearing her phlegmy throat.

"Actually, yes. Want some soda?" Kate asked.

She nodded, and waited for her secretary to unscrew the two liter Sprite bottle.

"Hope you don't mind. I put Alan in touch with Nikki, and she took Kimi in. She should be okay for a while. Small town. Nobody will recognize her there."

"Good." Nikki was Colleen's contact in North Carolina who adored her boots so much. She owned a small natural cosmetics company set on a rural farm. People might ask questions about the newcomer, but Nikki being who she was, she'd shake folks out of their line of questioning easily enough. Kimi would be okay there until her visiting visa expired, and then she'd have to make some tough choices.

Colleen understood Kimi's reluctance to go home in a way. She felt stifled there. Fettered. Like she had to live up to other people's expectations without actually knowing what her own were. Kimi was sick of pleasing other people when deep down inside, she was so unhappy. Hell of a way to live.

She'd felt that way at Markson Outfitters, sometimes.

Colleen took the warm soda Kate offered and sipped.

"Don't ya want to know what's going on at the farm?"

"It's just going to stress me out, and when I get stressed, I throw up. So, no."

"Tough. Gonna tell you anyway because that's what good secretaries do." She counted off on her fingers. "The books are a mess, Arfer is pining over you being gone ... "

"Liar."

"You're right. Arfer couldn't care less, but you really do need to go cut some checks. Contractors are waiting on deposits, and Alan keeps putting them off, telling them you haven't been into the office since last week. They're all understanding 'cause by now everyone in town knows you're knocked up. Alan hasn't exactly been coy about that."

"He and Daddy can have each other. Blabbermouths."

"Aw." Pixie rubbed Colleen's back, and gave her a little patronizing pat on the head. "Maybe it'll be good for your reputation. I know deep down inside you're a little pussy cat, but those folks don't know that. Cold Colleen becoming a mommy? Unfathomable."

"My own mother thinks so, too."

"Your mother probably thought it'd never happen. Between you and Jacob, the woman probably thought she'd die without having grandchildren."

"Great. I needed more drama in my life."

"I'm just being honest."

"Well, Daddy can go cut the checks if Alan is desperate. He has all the system passwords."

"Well, maybe Alan doesn't want Joe in the farm business. It's not Joe's farm anymore. It's Alan's and yours."

She groaned, and slowly rose to standing. When her head didn't swim, she started the short shuffle to the bathroom. "Enough."

"Least you could do is answer your phone, Colleen," Kate said.

"Why?" She closed the bathroom door and locked it.

Footsteps sounded in the hallway, and Kate called through the door, "Because you're hiding like your momma, and the Colleen I know doesn't hide. She sticks her chin out and takes her blows."

She sighed, flushed, and washed her hands before responding. "Colleen is so battered and bruised from taking blows for so long that she's brain-dead. Cold Colleen needs a vacation. She'll be back to work whenever her husband goes away."

"Open this door."

"No." She sat on the tub edge and crossed her arms over her belly.

"You do realize Pixie has a key to this door, right?"

"Why do you insist on torturing me? I'm getting enough of that from this alien life form growing inside me."

Kate wriggled the doorknob. When she spoke again, her voice was soft. "Colleen, come on, honey. We need you out in the world, not holed up in that bathroom. We need you at the farm."

"Oh, I thought it was Alan's farm."

"Don't sass me. I told you weeks ago you two were making a mess, and look at you now. There's something wrong with your generation, aren't I right, Pixie?"

From somewhere down the hall, Pixie called, "Yup."

"A few weeks ago, you said you'd like to buy him out some day. I want to know why you'd bother."

"Because I don't want to owe anyone anything."

"Oh, Colleen, you're giving this old lady heartburn. You're the mess-fixer, so fix this one. You're making it harder than it has to be."

"Easy for you to say," she whispered, but maybe Kate was right and she was making it hard. She was hiding because she was embarrassed. She hadn't been able to tell the difference between genuine affection and smooth talking, and had let a man exploit her at a time of unprecedented stress and weakness.

So, she was human after all. She wouldn't *dare* let herself feel guilty about that for a second longer.

She stood and turned the door lock.

When she pulled the door in, both Kate and Pixie were standing on the other side of it, waiting.

"I thought about bribing you with chocolate cake," Kate said, "but I didn't think you could keep it down. Please come back. If you and Alan need to have it out, go on and get it over with.

Work with him, Colleen. Do what you gotta, 'cause I would love more than anything to be a witness to the rebirth of Split Acres under your watch, girl. How sweet would it be knowing you took something that was run into the ground and made it soar again?"

She sniffled and dragged the sleeve of her bathrobe across her nose. "Pretty sweet," she admitted.

"So go do it."

She nodded and skulked past the two women in search of her shoes.

Pixie called down the hall, "Colleen?"

"Yeah?"

"You should shower, honey. Right now, you look less like the ball buster and more like the ball that rolled under a parked car and landed in a mud puddle."

"Oh."

CHAPTER TWENTY

"You've got to admit, it's hard for me not to be skeptical, Alan, under the circumstances." Sam Whitman paced in front of Alan's desk, raking his thin hair back from his forehead.

Alan had set up his office in the empty room adjacent to Colleen's, although at the moment, he mostly used it to store electrical components. He'd been helping the contractors block out wiring for the greenhouses, but if Colleen didn't come back soon, he'd have to write them a personal check. That'd make things messy, commingling his business and personal accounts. The farm's accountant would probably have a fit.

"I'm not sure what you expect me to do," he said.

Sam stopped pacing. "When's Joe going to be in the office next? I should take this up with him."

Right. And Joe would do nothing but say some pretty words and distract Sam from the topic at hand. It was good that Joe would be taking an extended hiatus from the farm and giving Alan and Colleen some time to get on their feet. After shoving his foot in his mouth and telling news he had no business to, Joe had been deservedly contrite and promised to give them some space. But that was *after* Alan's mother had laughed and crowed, "That'll make him stay put."

His father had cut his wife a steely gaze which she seemed wholly unaffected by... and then Mr. Prevost walked away. Alan had no idea what the long-term repercussions of his splintering off from the family business would be, but could only hope his parents didn't make things difficult.

"My father-in-law is on vacation from the farm. He won't return for at least a month."

"A month?" Sam cocked up a brow. "He was hardly here as it is. What's going on? Did he retire and not tell anyone?"

"I don't think Joe plans on retiring anytime soon."

Obfuscation. Alan had learned that little trick from Joe.

"So, tell me what *you* can do for me, Alan. You gotta do something for Emerald Tea. It was your sister on the front page of that paper, and now the folks over there are understandably miffed. Why didn't you tell them who you were when you applied?"

"Perhaps I wanted to be hired on the basis of something other than my last name. I don't believe in legacy treatment. I want to build my own reputation."

"But then you went and married into our competition next door!"

A feminine sigh from the doorway made Alan look up.

He stood at the sight of Colleen leaning against the frame in a dark pink maxi dress and pair of floral-print boots. The bags under her eyes looked heavy enough to tip her over, should she have the misfortunate of leaning the wrong way.

"Come on, Sam," she said. "Let's not be disingenuous. Calling us the competition is flattering, but the last time our two farms were on the same level was probably when I was thirteen. Our crop lists barely overlap anymore. If we were to set up two farmer's market stalls side by side, there'd be limited duplication. Besides, people don't choose between Split Acres apples and Emerald Tea Farm apples. Yours are organic. Ours aren't. They're shelved completely separately at the grocery store. What are you really afraid of?"

His girl, she didn't hash her words. Why waste time dithering?

Sam fixed his stare on her and seemed lost for words for a moment.

Good.

He cleared his throat and looked back to Alan. "I didn't want to be the one to say it, but your presence here is suspicious. You need to be careful."

"That sounds like a threat," Colleen said, not willing to be ignored. "And I don't appreciate it. If you may recall, I've had my truck murdered and one of my farm buildings met a suspiciously untimely end in the past month, not to mention all the other dreadfully expensive Band-Aids I've had to slap onto things around here. I don't toss blame around, because it's a waste of my time, and I've got things to do. I'm going to suck it up and forge on because that's the only guarantee I have that things will get done."

"I'm surprised at you, Colleen. What you're doing is tantamount to sleeping with the enemy. We've been your friends for so long, and, I mean, the Prevosts ... "

She tipped her chin down in warning. "I respect you, Sam, and Richard, too, but you need to be careful about slinging allegations around about my family. It's hard for me not to be offended. I'm very different from my father in a lot of ways, but one way we're similar is that we hold grudges. You don't want me to hold a grudge, now do you?"

Alan kept his tongue still. There was no way Colleen could know what the Prevosts were or were not capable of—what they'd done to grab and hold onto their success—but she was making her choice known. She was stating her allegiance to Alan, putting up a public front of solidarity when in truth, she had to be fuming on the inside.

Why else would she run and hide from him?

Could he really blame her? He knew she'd be angry, but he had wanted to tell her everything in his own time. He wanted her to fall madly in love with him and need him so much, that even through the anger, she'd forgive him for it all ... and want him as much as he wanted her.

And, God, he wanted her more than anything, including the farm.

Damn the farm. He half wished he'd never seen it.

Sam blew out a sigh. "Will you have Kate call me and let me know when Joe is scheduled to return? This mess has been going on too long. No reason why old friends shouldn't be able to come to terms."

What terms, exactly? He didn't ask, and apparently Colleen didn't care because she just nodded and eased out of the doorway to let Sam pass.

After the front door whooshed open, and creaked shut, Colleen gave Alan a hard stare then left his office.

Just like that.

Was she kidding him?

"Colleen." He followed her the short distance to her office where she stabbed her computer on and stared at the monitor as the machine booted up.

Her face was stony, but that hand draped over her computer mouse shook.

He sighed. "Colleen. Please."

She typed in her password and watched the screen. "I understand you have some checks that need to be cut. Can you bring me the invoices?"

The invoices? They had a huge boulder dangling over their heads, and she wanted to talk about invoices.

He shook his head. "We can deal with the bills later. Where have you been?"

"Why?"

Why?

What kind of question was that? Because she was his wife and he'd worried she hadn't come home. He didn't think she'd buy that line, though. Not coming from him.

"Because I bought a blueberry pie and didn't have anyone to share it with."

She rolled her eyes. "If only I could eat pie."

"I heard you were in the hospital. You should have called me."

She drummed her fingertips on the desktop. "The invoices, Alan. Give them to me."

It may have been his imagination, but suddenly the room seemed to freeze over.

Clenching his fists at his sides, he turned on his heel and strode from her office, up the hallway, over the dog, and paused in front of Kate's desk.

Kate looked at him over her reading glasses.

"I thought you talked to her."

The secretary closed her eyes and nodded. "Mmm hmm. I did."

"She doesn't seem … particularly crusty to you?"

"Of course she does. Not my problem, though."

"You said you'd help."

She pushed a stack of invoices across her desktop. "I did help. She's here, isn't she? Did you want me to do *all* the work? I don't get paid enough for that."

He ground the heels of his palms against his closed eyes. "God."

She lowered a voice to a whisper and said, "Hey, if she were easy, she wouldn't be worth having, right?"

"Right. But knowing that doesn't make the situation any less frustrating."

"What do you want, a pep talk?"

"No. How about a magic arrow?"

"Eh." She waved a dismissive hand at him. "Take your bills."

He took them and walked back down the hall with a sigh.

Colleen didn't even look up when he slipped the papers onto her desktop.

"That should be all of them."

"Great. Need anything else?" She slid her chair back, bent to open a desk drawer, and withdrew a stack of laser printer checks.

"Yes, I need you to look at me. *Acknowledge* me."

She looked at him, and there was so much malice in her eyes, he regretted asking for it.

He deserved it and knew it, so he held her gaze. Took it. Made it his penance for lying to her.

She stood with the checks and walked them to the printer. After slipping them into the tray, she returned to her seat and studied the pile of invoices. "When's all this work set to start?"

He raked his fingers through his hair and pulled. "Can we not just talk about business as if there aren't more pressing issues at hand than when the contractors will start putting up the greenhouse walls?"

"But the farm is the most important thing, isn't it? Can't make money in our current state. Have to press on."

"Colleen … "

"What?"

"You're making this hard for me, and I understand the compulsion. I really do. But please believe me when I say I never meant to hurt you. I never wanted it to be like this. I never thought I'd fall in love with you."

"Love?" Coming out her mouth, the word was dry. Bitter. "Love, you say? Right. I need to get some air. Feeling nauseous."

She hurried to the door, looking a bit green around the gills, and his shoulders fell.

"That went well."

CHAPTER TWENTY-ONE

Alan followed at a respectful distance to the picnic table. When she sat, he took a seat on the same side, a couple of feet away, watching her.

"You don't have to fluff up my feelings, Alan. I'm here. Working. You can do what you want."

"I'm doing what I want to be doing right now. We need to have this conversation."

"Maybe we should have had this conversation a few weeks ago. Maybe I could have been talked into a partnership. I'm a reasonable woman most of the time." She looked at him, and to his credit, he didn't flinch. Just watched.

"I happen to agree with you, Colleen. We should have. I should have told you everything, and I'm sorry for that. At one point, I didn't know what I really wanted, beyond being here in this place. But then I realized this place wasn't worth anything if you didn't come with it."

"Bullshit. I'm not a commodity."

"No, you're a woman with a tough outer shell I've been trying to crack for weeks, and I fear I'm responsible for its current hardness."

"You would be right." Some of that crustiness she could ascribe to the baby, but the baby was at least half Alan's fault, too.

Washington was a community property state, after all.

"We have to work together," he said, touching her knee.

Her impulse was to pull away, but she drew in a breath and endured it. Because with her anger at the moment, that's what dealing with Alan required. Endurance.

The one man she opened herself up to in years, and she'd picked a doozy. She'd never had a problem keeping business and pleasure separate, so why had she started now? Now everything was irreparably entangled. She couldn't cut ties from Alan even if she tried. Even if she left the farm, and she wouldn't do that.

"Were you going to tell me about the baby, or was that going to be another secret for you to keep with Pixie and Kate? Like our marriage?"

For a brief moment, the ice around her heart softened, and then she turned the freezer back up. He had no right. "You want to talk about secrets, Alan? That's so rich coming from you. The man I thought I could trust as a business partner whose intentions all along were to edge me out of my own farm. "

"Half a farm, Colleen. And now you have a *whole* farm, minus a couple of shares."

"No. *You* have a whole farm. It was your money. You're the one with all the power because I'll never be able to pay you back. It's just that my name is on all the paperwork with yours and will be until this sham of a marriage is dissolved. I'll get it on its feet because that was my goal all along, and then I don't know what'll happen. I guess we'll be happily divorced by then."

"The hell we will be. I'm going to make you stick this out until you know in your heart I'm not lying to you. I don't care how much I have to work to get us there. I swear to you, from now on, I'll never make you regret trusting me. I know how valuable that gift is."

Was this really happening? The entire exchange seemed surreal, given her very recent conversation with her former boss. Some of the last words she'd said to the man were "I love my husband," and at the time, she'd meant them. Still meant them, no matter how angry he made her.

"What do you want, Alan?" she asked, her voice a tired whisper. "Don't make this baby just another business transaction for you. Another acquisition." Placing her hands on her belly, she tried to implore him with her expression. "For all I know, this ball of cells may be the only chance I get to be a mother. I don't want this ... this *baby* to be the cause of acrimony."

He raked his hands through his hair again. "This is a bloody mess. I don't think I'm communicating very well. I thought what I wanted would be clear to you, or else I would have gone about this a different way."

"What are you talking about?"

"The farm, Colleen. Yes, at first I wanted to buy you out, but then I realized this may be a one-shot deal for me. You may be my one chance at having a family—dear lord, a *family*—of my own. I thought maybe I could leverage the farm to secure not just my future but *ours*."

"What?"

He removed the hand from her knee and slid closer, slowly, and wrapped his left arm around her waist.

She turned her knees slightly toward him. "What are you saying, Alan?"

"When you said weeks ago that you were ready for your father to retire, I started thinking about how I could help make that happen for you. I had my plans, yes, but I wanted you to see some of yours come to fruition as well. You better than anyone know how much work this farm needs to make it profitable."

"Years of hard work and spending more than the income."

"Yes, and I'm fine with spending the money because one day all that stress will be worth it, and we'll have something to show for it."

"We'll?"

He nodded. "I don't want to do this by myself. I don't want this dream to come to fruition if you can't be in it."

He reached a tentative right hand across his body and folded his fingers around her left hand. He turned her hand over so her palm faced up. Dropping her ring onto it, he met her gaze. "Found that in the flowers."

A laughed escaped her throat, and she couldn't help it. "I threw it."

"I guessed. Please, Colleen." He closed her fingers over the ring, and she stared down at their entwined hands.

"I do love you, Colleen. Maybe you didn't believe me when I said it before, but I do. I'm sorry I hurt you. If I could take it all back, I would. But here we are now, right?"

"Yeah, I guess so."

"Do you love me?" He gave her hand a squeeze.

She laughed. "I've loved you for almost as long as I've hated you."

"That long, huh?" He smiled and skimmed his thumb over her hand.

"The Whitmans must think we're behind all the bad stuff. That we're trying to run them down like this farm is."

"I don't care. We'll deal with it until it all blows away, and your brother will keep heads cool, I hope. Wonder if he regrets selling us his piece of the farm."

"If he does, it's probably not for financial reasons." God, what must Jacob be thinking? She was his *sister*, and she'd gone and gotten married without so much as a heads-up. It'd break her heart if he'd ever do the same to her. But, he had a good head on his shoulders, so no matter who he picked, she'd trust he made the right choice. Even if it meant eloping.

Alan's fingers squeezed around hers, pulling her back into the conversation. "You'll move in with me?"

He brushed his hand up and down her left side, awaiting her response.

"Yes."

"Then I'll confess one more thing."

"What?"

"I killed your bed. Hoped if you were uncomfortable enough, I'd lure you to mine."

"Creative." She pressed her hands over her eyes and laughed. If that wasn't romantic, she didn't know what was.

"Well, what's more, I also caused that hot water heater leak."

That made her pull back. "What?"

He put up his hands. "Same deal."

She narrowed her eyes. "Anything else I should blame you for? My truck, perhaps?"

"No, I'd never ruin an engine that way. Makes it harder to melt down the scrap metal. I did tinker with your old desk chair, though."

"That's cold."

"Yeah. I'm in good company."

She sighed, propped her head on his shoulder, and studied her plain gold wedding band.

"I've got better rings for you. In my drawer. You should have better rings. I can imagine the talk with people knowing my net worth and them thinking I skimped."

"I don't care."

"I don't either, but everyone else will. If they're going to talk about us, I'd rather it not be for that. You can wear all three."

"Pretty sure that's more jewelry than I've ever worn in my entire life."

"Gold on that finger suits you." He wrapped his arm around her back and let his fingers graze her belly.

"What's going to happen now?" she asked as she pushed her ring back on.

"Well, we hold our breath until we hear the baby's heartbeat, line up our contractors as planned, and then we wade out into the muck of public opinion. Together."

"Muck. Yeah. Good thing I have lots of boots."

A Sneak Peek from Emerald Springs Legacy Book Three
(From *Chad's Chance* by Elley Arden)

The end of the day was made for a cold glass of beer.

All the scrubbing, rinsing, lifting, and sweating made Jen's limbs limp and her mouth dry. It was a good kind of whipped, the kind that left no room for regrets or loneliness. In fact, when the hoppy flavor nipped her tongue and inner cheeks, it wiped away thought and left behind a sense of satisfaction. She still couldn't believe she could make such a beautiful beverage from scratch.

Jen sighed as she reached a heavy arm over her head and felt around the dark recesses of her locker shelf for her brewmaster gloves.

"I need to talk to you."

Her stomach heaved on an internal groan. *What now?*

Felix was a beady-eyed creep, who only came sniffing around the backend of the microbrewery when he wanted to cause trouble.

"In my office," he said, spinning on the heels of his snake-skin loafers and using stubby-legged strides to propel him from the break room.

Great. She slammed shut her locker and followed him, her pink rubber boots making faint squeaks as she marched. The scent of fried food and burnt pizza crust wafted down the main hall, adding to her stomach's discomfort. All she wanted was a beer.

"Come in so I can close the door."

She glanced over her shoulder into the hallway, wishing to pull a passing waitress into the room. It wasn't wise to engage Felix without a witness.

When the hallway appeared like a gaping black hole, she rolled back her shoulders, lifted her chin and exhaled. "I prefer we leave the door open."

"Have it your way," he sneered, and then he deposited his lumpy body into the ridiculously large leather chair behind his cluttered desk. "Chavez, we have to let you go."

Air ripped from her lungs. "Let me go where?"

He tossed her a lopsided look filled with pity. "We can't afford to keep two brewmasters, so we have to let you go."

"You're firing me." The words scraped against her throat until she thought she tasted blood.

Shit. She always figured she'd be the one to get the last laugh around here ... when she quit.

"Bruno has more experience."

Barely. He was ten years older, but he had only a year of additional brewing experience on Jen. What really mattered to Felix was that Bruno had a penis.

"Bruno's IPA tastes like piss," Jen countered, wringing her hands and stepping one foot backward.

Part of her wanted to go. Part of her wanted to stay. She could fight this. With Felix's subtle sexual harassment and Alicia's toxic jealousy over any female worker who was in his company too long, it shouldn't be hard to get an employment lawyer to take the case.

A long and vindictive lawsuit flashed before her eyes. Why would she want to waste energy fighting them? To get her job back? Felix and Alicia wouldn't be going anywhere, and as long as they owned the place, Jen's life here would be hell.

"Gather your things, and I'll escort you out."

"No need," she hissed.

As she stormed back to the break room, emotion overtook her, clogging her throat, burning her eyes. The blockage made her heart beat faster. She'd worked her ass off for this job—literally— sweating body fat in an un-air-conditioned brew house, and this was her thanks. Those serving vessels out there were filled with *her* creations.

Jerking open her locker, she bit hard into the side of her cheek to keep the tears in check. She was not going to cry. Not here. That would prove the very thing Felix and Alicia had been worried about all along—a female brewmaster was too weak.

She peeled the Milwaukee Brewer's schedule magnet off the back of the door and yanked her Colorado sweatshirt from its hook. Her purse was barely big enough for the checkbook-sized wallet and sunglass case she insisted on carrying around, but still she stuffed the magnet and as much of the hooded sweatshirt as possible into it.

She slammed her locker again, but opened it back up and reached for her gloves on the overhead shelf. Empty. She must've left them in the brew house.

For the third time she slammed her locker, opened it, and slammed it a final time. It was better than screaming *motherfucker* at the top of her lungs for the restaurant full of patrons to hear. Oh, she'd scream it, but she'd wait until she got home.

Storming out the other side of the break room with her weighed-down purse in hand, she chewed the inside of her cheek and fought the fury. She'd like nothing better than to stalk back into the office and launch at Felix, clawing his eyes out. It would be satisfying, but it would be ugly.

Jen had firsthand experience with violence. Giving into unbridled anger where a man was concerned would make her no better than her mother, so she would refrain—somehow. She'd bottle it up tight, get the hell out and find another way to release the angry energy that was eating her alive.

When she threw open the door to the brew house, Jen froze. Earthy scents hit her nose, relaxing her raised-back posture, calming her pounding heart. She dropped her purse at the door's threshold and stepped across, like a Catholic schoolgirl headed for confession.

Brewing was her religion; it cleansed her soul.

She cried—just a tear or two—because she didn't know when she'd see something this magnificent again.

High-polished silver vessels rose from the floor like the staggered pipes of a church organ. Her breath caught, creating a painful blockage in her throat. She'd brewed her last batch of Lovely Lady here. Had she known it was going to be her last, she'd have paid more attention, made damn sure every detail was committed to memory. And she would've tasted it—over and over again—until she couldn't swallow without thinking of her trademark honey ale.

She took in the room where she spent most of the last two years, the sense of melancholy heavy on her shoulders. As much as she hated the owners of this establishment, she'd have put up with worse if that was the only way for her make beer. Without it, life seemed impossible. Something else her mother's many men taught her. There was nothing like a tall one to tame the savage beast.

A pair of purple brewer's gloves on the top metal step caught Jen's eye. She'd come for those, not for gloomy memories. There would be other jobs. Maybe not in Seattle. Maybe not in a microbrewery with cutting-edge equipment like this. But there would be other brewmaster jobs.

She'd do whatever she had to do to find one.

• • •

Chad accepted the billfold and a to-go jug of Lovely Lady Honey Ale from the waitress.

"Thanks so much," she said, smiling. "Hope you stop back soon."

He would.

This escape from the chaos back in Emerald Springs had been nice. Between breaking up a fistfight at the diner and navigating Dad's impending retirement wedged Adam's upcoming wedding. The fistfight and ensuing bad publicity aside, Chad was trying to remain positive and supportive. Dad deserved to slowdown, and Adam deserved to be happy. But getting from Point A to Point B meant too much family and family business drama. Chad didn't have the taste for that. He still didn't know if he'd ever acquire a taste for settling down and being responsible like he'd promised Mom he would do.

He preferred the taste of a damn good beer.

Touching his pinky to the cold glass jug the waitress left behind, he wondered how long a sixty-four ounce growler would last him. A couple weeks? Dad wouldn't be officially retired by then, and Adam wouldn't be married, yet, so Chad would definitely be throwing back a few. The good thing was, when he ran out, he could escape to Seattle again. Next time, though, he'd visit the microbrewery without Billy. The glazed-over look on his best friend's face told Chad this outing had been too much too soon.

"Everything okay at home?" Chad asked as he signed the slip and returned his credit card to his wallet.

"I'm telling you. It's the cutest thing. She smiles when she sleeps. Molly says she's smiling at angels." Billy held his cell phone inches from Chad's face.

The newborn looked more like a hairless monkey than the offspring of Billy and Molly, but once again Chad said she was cute. He'd said it at least a dozen times today—even when the critter in question puked all over his shoulder. Thank God he'd been wearing one of those towels.

As Billy returned his attention to the cell phone, Chad turned his head, dropped his gaze and sniffed his shoulder making sure...

When he glanced up, something pink beyond the glass that separated the restaurant from the brew house caught his eye. *Boots?*

He followed the girly boots to a pair of shapely thighs and an ass that made his back straighten. "Who the hell is that?"

Billy turned his head and said, "Probably the brewmaster" without a hint of interest.

That was okay. Chad had enough interest for both of them. His breath thickened as she bent over to grab a pair of gloves, testing the limits of those denim seams, and then she faced the restaurant. Surrounded by steel, dressed in a black tee and jeans, with hair the color of a midnight sky cascading from a spot high on her head, she commanded the attention of every vibrating atom in his body.

She was gorgeous. And then she was gone.

Chad blinked, and Billy's voice registered in his ears. "You know what I mean?"

Chad didn't have a clue. He opened his mouth for bigger breaths. What the hell...

"Hey, man. You okay?" Billy asked. "You're bright red."

Chad nodded. He lifted the growler of beer as he stood with purpose. "I wonder if they give tours. I'd like a tour."

"Nah, I can't. I...it's been three hours already. I gotta get home." Billy held his cell phone in one hand and his keys in the other.

Chad searched the restaurant behind Billy with hyperactive eyes. "Yeah, yeah. I understand."

He'd be back inside the building before Billy left his parking spot.

As they weaved through the dining room to the exit, Chad kept one eye on Billy so he didn't run the poor guy over and one eye on the brew house. Would she show up there again? Would she have reason to come out here?

"I appreciate you making the drive up and taking me out," Billy said as he held the glass door open.

"My pleasure," Chad said, deciding to devote the next sixty seconds to heartily seeing off his best friend. "You're a lucky man."

He meant it. Just because he wasn't cut out for the responsibility of marriage and family didn't mean he couldn't appreciate the trait in a friend. Now, the mini-van? That was harder to accept. Chad couldn't even ride in it.

Standing alongside the metallic blue hallmark of family life, they hugged—mostly chest bumped—and back slapped. "Take care of those girls," Chad said.

"Will do. Drive safe. Thanks again."

For a brief second Billy wore the same silly smile he had worn in the huddle minutes before he launched off the line with reckless abandon, wreaking havoc on helpless defenders intent on sacking Chad ... but then it was gone. With serious lines carved into his forehead, he focused on the side-view mirrors, looked over his shoulder enough times to give Chad a sympathetic crick in the neck, and edged the mini-van out of the too-tight space.

Cautious. See? That right there was why Chad would never make a good husband let alone a father. It was exactly why he was struggling to find a comfortable place in the family business. That constant awareness of other people's lives depending on you cut a man's ability to take risks. Hell, it eliminated them. The mere thought had him gasping for air.

Chad liked risks. The risks made life fun. But since Mom died he hadn't been able to take a single chance without the repercussions throttling him.

"Shit."

The expletive came from behind him followed by a dull thud.

He turned around to find the woman in pink boots crouched on the pavement amid what looked like a sweatshirt, rubber gloves and the contents of her purse.

"Let me help," he said, setting the growler of beer on the pavement, unable to believe his luck.

He picked up the object closest to him, a Milwaukee Brewer's fridge magnet, and chuckled. "You don't see many of these around here."

Brown eyes, wet and wide, lifted to his face. "It was a gift," she said, her voice raspy.

If he thought she was beautiful inside the brewery, then he had no idea what to call it out here. In the early evening sun, flecks of red emerged from her onyx hair. She blinked, studying him with murky eyes. *Wounded.* Lashes that were too long to be real clumped together with what appeared to be tears.

"Are you okay?" he whispered, not even recognizing the sound of his voice.

She nodded and slicked her pink tongue between pale lips. "Always."

Blood hammered through his veins straight to his crotch.

He grabbed a pen and a butterscotch candy off the pavement and held them in his open hand.

"Thank you," she said, scraping her clean nails over his palm as she retrieved the items.

His jaw clenched as pleasant chills radiated from his hand over his body. He couldn't seem to keep his attention focused on anything other than his body's insane reaction to this woman.

"I like your boots," he blurted, hoping the inane statement would reverse this crazy train.

She didn't look at him as she stood. Instead she hung her head, and he felt like a giant jerk for being turned on when she was obviously upset.

He was seconds away from asking if there was someone he could call to help her out when she jabbed a pointed finger at his feet.

"You need to pick that up and get it to your car." The rasp in her voice turned biting.

When he didn't move, she jabbed again. "Do you know how hot that pavement is? Would you set it on a stove top?" Her eyes never left the growler. "Treat it right or don't drink it at all."

Chad bent over and lifted the glass jug of beer. Her fierce protection of the item reminded him of where he first saw her.

"You're the brewmaster, aren't you?"

An agonizing sound stuck in her throat and she shook her head. "Not anymore."

She sidestepped him. Her boots made the silliest *thud, thud, squeak* against the pavement, and her ass swung like a porch swing in a windstorm.

He jogged after her. Had she been fired? It would explain the tears.

"Hey, you're upset. Let me help."

Her initial glance could've frozen Puget Sound, but then she looked at the growler in his hand again, and her striking features softened.

"Okay. You want to help? You can give me that," she said, coming to a stop behind his Jeep.

With her sculpted eyebrows lifted and her lips pursed, she looked serious, like they were negotiating something much more valuable than a twenty-dollar growler of beer. He didn't know how old she was, twenty-five maybe, but the shadows in her eyes told him life experience made up for whatever she lacked in age.

Whether it was a good idea or not, he wanted to help her lighten up.

Looking at the beer, Chad shrugged. "I don't know. You're asking a lot. I drove all the way to Seattle for this beer." Not exactly true. He was leaving things out, like the part about Billy's baby. Then again, he left out the part about wanting this beer when he offered to take Billy to dinner in the first place. What the other didn't know...

An odd smile lifted one side of her mouth. "Really?"

That half-smile lit a flame. Chad hitched his free thumb in his jean pocket and grinned through a blast of body heat hot enough to cause beads of sweat on his back. "Really. It's the best honey ale I've ever tasted."

She nodded, sniffed, and glanced above him. Then she smiled—big and bold. When she looked at him again, the tip of her tongue touched the tip of her snow-white teeth. "It is, isn't it?"

Zap! His brain primed his body with all sorts of bad ideas, and she stood there smiling at him with a twinkle in her sultry eyes like she was game for every damn one.

A reasonable man would give her the beer and walk away, but not a cooped-up risk-taker like Chad.

"We could share it," he said, knowing he could be reading her wrong. Maybe she wasn't interested. Maybe…

She snatched the growler out of his hand. "Follow me."

To purchase this ebook and learn more about the author, *click here*.

The Emerald Springs Legacy Series

Follow the Whitman and Sanders families in their continuing saga as they confront old rivalries and discover new love while protecting their legacy at the Emerald Tea Farm. Look for these upcoming installments in this exciting new continuity series from Crimson Romance:

Adam's Ambition by Monica Tillery

Colleen's Choice by Holley Trent

Chad's Chance by Elley Arden

Daniel's Decision by Nicole Flockton

Ashley's Allegiance by Robyn Neeley

To learn more about the Emerald Springs series, visit our website for more details, author interviews, and a special free prequel story.

www.ingramcontent.com/pod-product-compliance
Lightning Source LLC
Chambersburg PA
CBHW010638100726
47900CB00011B/2872